PROTECT ME

(A Katie Winter FBI Suspense Thriller—Book 8)

Molly Black

Molly Black

Bestselling author Molly Black is author of the MAYA GRAY FBI suspense thriller series, comprising nine books (and counting); of the RYLIE WOLF FBI suspense thriller series, comprising six books (and counting); of the TAYLOR SAGE FBI suspense thriller series, comprising six books (and counting); and of the KATIE WINTER FBI suspense thriller series, comprising nine books (and counting).

An avid reader and lifelong fan of the mystery and thriller genres, Molly loves to hear from you, so please feel free to visit www.mollyblackauthor.com to learn more and stay in touch.

ISBN: 978-1-0943-9554-8

PROLOGUE

The trunk of the tall sugar maple tree stretched high above Gavin Barnes. Below him, the ground fell away, forty feet down, a dangerous drop. But that was all part of the challenge, the excitement. You literally could die doing this dare, and that was why they did it.

It was better not to look down. Looking down made his stomach twist. Up was where they were going. As high as possible. He needed to beat his friend Mike, climbing determinedly below him, but ready to pass him if Gavin paused, or froze.

"You're going slowly," Mike teased breathlessly. "Getting scared?"

"Me? Never!"

Gavin grabbed the branch above him, hoping to get a lead on his friend. But as he pushed himself up, his foot slipped and he felt a moment of sheer terror, a moment as he imagined losing his grip on the tree's rough bark, and falling down, tumbling through the air, crashing into the forest below.

He tightened his grip, but his hands were trembling. He could feel the rough bark biting into his palms.

He clung to the branch, taking a moment to stabilize himself before wedging his foot more securely.

"You okay? Did you slip?" Mike asked, amusement and anxiety combined in his tone.

"I'm great," Gavin said, though his voice shook. "Just getting up some speed to leave you behind."

"Thought you were losing your nerve for a minute there," Mike teased.

Gavin pulled himself up, panting. He had to get past the near miss, and not think about what could have happened.

"Catch up, Mike!" he called out.

Then he grabbed the next branch, began to pull himself up.

Now that he was moving again, back in his rhythm, Gavin felt a rush of excitement as he climbed. The wind rushed past his ears as he pulled himself up the tree. It was good to be climbing, away from the boring old town below.

1

Of all the trees in this thickly forested part of northern Minnesota, this was one of the tallest, and the reason why they'd chosen it for their competition today.

It was spring, but the sun-dappled forest felt cold, and the wind tugged at Gavin's short, dark hair as he ascended. It always felt breezier in the upper branches, and yet again, he was reminded of that slip. If the wind got up, it could pull you right out of the tree. He thought for a moment how it would feel to fall, not just a slip of the foot, but yards and yards, tumbling down.

Don't think about it, he warned himself. Freezing up now would be a bad idea. A really bad decision. He didn't want to end up like a cat, stranded high in the branches, too scared to get down again. But now that they were getting higher, the tree was starting to sway, as if its upper branches and leafy canopy couldn't hold the weight of two teenage boys on a dare.

Perhaps it couldn't, he thought, with another flash of fear. Or perhaps it just felt that way. For a second, he imagined he could hear the cracking of a branch.

"You know you're going more slowly than me," Mike called. He grabbed Gavin's ankle and Gavin yelled in fright.

"Don't do that, man! Are you crazy?"

"Don't let me catch up," Mike warned. "You're slowing down!"

"Am not," Gavin called back.

"Chicken."

It was Mike who had dared them both to climb it. But it was Gavin who was struggling now.

He'd been doing fine until that slip. Now that he was back up, climbing with his heart racing, that scare was making him more aware of the distance between him and the ground.

He began climbing again, concentrating on the bark beneath his palms, the rough surface that was making him slip, making his hands sweat even more. And now a gust of wind, swirling through the treetops, caught at the branch under Gavin's hand and it began to shake.

And then, he saw something that distracted him. Something exciting, that motivated him to get past his fear and push on, push ahead.

"Hey!" he called excitedly.

"What?" Mike asked.

"I can see the machinery now! I can actually watch where they're clearing the trees."

A couple hundred yards away, the incessant drone of the machines at work provided a noisy background to the usually quiet forest. An area of the woods was being cleared for development. It was a massive project. Soon, their small town wouldn't be so small anymore. It might even be less boring, or so Gavin hoped.

"I want to see! But we better not let them see us. I'm sure we'll get into trouble," Mike warned. "We're not supposed to be near the construction site at all."

"I'm sure they're too busy to worry about us," Gavin said, but he kept his head down all the same, made sure he didn't poke it out beyond the thick, leafy branches. But if he got up another yard, he'd have a great view. He might even be able to watch as an actual tree got felled and went crashing to the floor. That would be something! He could film it. He had his phone in his pocket.

And then, under his foot, the worst happened.

The branch he had all his weight on, snapped. It was a sharp crack that made him jump like he was shot, made him shriek out in fright

He could feel the branch slipping beneath him, feel it giving way, and he knew that if he stayed, he'd fall and there would be no stopping from crashing down from the mighty height he'd climbed to.

He reached out, grabbing for the next limb, but that was slick with damp leaves and he couldn't get a grip on it. He felt himself slipping. I'm going to fall, he thought, and the real terror of it hit him.

"Please, Mike!" he called. "Get me!"

He could hear Mike gasping for air as he struggled to climb up towards him.

"Hurry!" Gavin urged. He reached out and grasped a thin branch, at a precarious angle, feeling a bolt of fear that this one would break, too.

"Hang in there!" Mike shouted. His friend grabbed his ankle again, this time pushing up, giving him the purchase he needed, but not enough.

He felt the branch he was hanging from move, quiver. He was going to fall. Gavin cried out as he felt himself start to slip again. He clamped his hands onto the branch like a man on a sinking ship.

Reaching up, almost blind with panic, he grabbed at something else. Another pale, slim branch, hoping that this one would offer more stability.

But it didn't feel like a branch. It was soft, cold, and flexible. And it, too, moved when he grabbed it.

3

It lurched downward, and he saw that what he'd thought was a branch was an arm.

"There's an arm here!" he cried out, hearing his own voice high with fear.

"What? You're kidding me, right?" But Mike's voice sounded scared too, now, picking up on the panic he could hear in his friend's.

It was an arm. He hadn't been hallucinating. A cold, pale arm, with a hand at the end. A hand with stiff, cold fingers that jerked down toward him.

Gavin began to scream in terror, trying to get down, moving his hands, adjusting his grip, grabbing out at anything he could except for that awful, impossible thing. He kicked Mike in the head by accident, clumsy with terror, and heard his friend shout in pain.

"We need to get down, man, we need to get down, this is crazy, there's a dead person here! A dead person! Mike, get down! Get out!"

But it was too late.

Dislodged, the body slid further. It slipped and lurched into his view.

And, now shrieking in panic, clinging to the leafy branches without even feeling his hands, Gavin came face to face with the corpse. The stuff of nightmares, a dead woman in the tree. He'd touched her, he had pulled her arm, and now she was slipping jerkily down from the canopy hiding place.

A sheet-white face slid down into his view. Tangled blonde hair spilled over his skin. And wide, sightless blue eyes stared into his own.

CHAPTER ONE

Katie Winter scrambled over the rocky trail. The stones felt hard and unforgiving under her boots. Weeds and shrubs tangled over the faint pathway. Her breath clouded in the chilly air, and the skies were as gray as a grave.

The area was remote, mountainous, and harsh. But as she trod the slippery path, hope flared in her heart that it might lead her to her sister.

Was this where Josie had been taken, after her tragic disappearance sixteen years ago? Was she even still alive, and was there the faintest hope that Katie might find her?

"I'm here for you. I'm on my way," she said to herself, wondering if her twin could sense her frantic determination to find her. "I never gave up on you, Josie. Ever. If you're here, I'll get to you. I'm just sorry it took me so long."

The harsh terrain she was hiking through was a few miles south of the U.S.-Canada border, in one of the wildest areas of New York State. The closest small town was a tiny hamlet named Clare.

The day was overcast and although not snowy, the weather was unpleasant for early spring. Cold rain was falling, lifting only briefly to lighten the heavy gloom. Katie wiped it away from her face, pulling her jacket's hood over her head, even though her shoulder-length, brown hair was already drenched.

"I had to track him down," she said aloud to her twin, through numb lips. "It wasn't easy. We didn't know what had happened. Our parents didn't want to know, and I wasn't able to find out. My first lead came from a convicted killer, Josie, can you believe it? He was the one who told me he'd seen Gabriel Rath approaching you, while you were unconscious on the riverbank after your kayak capsized. Nobody else saw or suspected Gabriel at the time. Everyone thought Everton, the killer, had murdered you. But then, I couldn't find Gabriel. That took longer than I thought it would."

But at last she had done it. She'd gotten the lead she was hoping for. The one she hoped might take her to the strange, bearded man who had been on the riverbank at the time of Josie's kayaking accident.

5

Gabriel Rath had not been seen in town after that incident. Nobody knew where he'd gone, apart from one person. His ex-landlady, Mrs. Ingham. She'd been one of the chattiest people in town, as well as the nosiest. She had found out from her tenant that he planned to move elsewhere sometime. That conversation must have happened long before he had the opportunity to take Josie.

But Mrs. Ingham was no longer living in town when Katie had followed that lead; she was with her extended family off the grid. Katie had to wait for impatient weeks until she came back into town.

Then, finally, she'd received the call she had been waiting and hoping for. But it had not given her precise information.

Mrs. Ingham hadn't known the details. She'd racked her brains for the memories of long ago, and told Katie that as far as she recalled, he'd said he was building a cabin about twenty miles to the west of Clare, and that he was going to move there when he was ready. It was very remote, he'd told her. Very isolated, with nobody else around. He was starting a new life there when his cabin was built, he'd said.

Katie knew why he'd made the decision to leave when he did. She was sure she knew why.

Because he'd taken Josie. He had a captured woman. He was holding her prisoner, stealing her life.

A few months before he'd taken Josie, Gabriel Rath had sent Mrs. Ingham a picture which she'd showed to Katie. A small, partially constructed cabin hidden in a copse of tall pine trees, bordering a narrow creek.

Katie had stared at that picture for hours when Mrs. Ingham had forwarded it to her, etching the scene into her mind.

Then, using a map and her best navigation ability, Katie had located the approximate coordinates where this cabin must be.

And now, as she scrambled over the dangerous terrain, she hoped she'd find it.

The land was steep, and it hadn't been maintained. There were no hiking trails through the area. It was exactly the kind of place where somebody like Gabriel Rath would hide away. Rough, treacherous terrain. Harsh and unforgiving. Nobody to hear if Josie screamed. A hand-built place where he could keep her locked away.

Or so Katie imagined.

She knew she had to be prepared for the fact that her sister had succumbed to her injuries at the time, and that Gabriel Rath had fled with nothing more than a chilly corpse for company.

Or that she'd died since then. Murdered by him, or injured while trying to escape him. Katie knew Josie would not have accepted her fate. Not her twin. Even at sixteen, she would have had the strength and the smarts to try to flee him.

But if she'd gotten away alive, she would have come home. Katie didn't doubt that. Josie hadn't, and that meant, perhaps, she was still there. Unable to escape, but still planning, still fighting, still hoping.

Katie hoped the search would lead to her sister, that the trail wouldn't go cold. She had to trust in her map reading and calculations to be sure she was on the right track.

Rough stones slipped beneath her feet. Her ankles turned on the sharp edges of the rocks, forcing her to curb her impatience and step carefully. She was grateful, at least, that the rain was light, and not coming down in sheets.

She checked her map and the GPS again, doing the calculations, feeling a twinge of anxiety, because by now she should have seen it. There was only one creek in the area. It was wider than it had looked in the photo but Katie guessed that was because it was swollen by the spring rains.

But the cabin should be here. It should be within sight by now.

Katie frowned.

She'd reached the only copse of wood in the rugged, mountainous area. The only place that resembled the photo she'd seen.

The mountains stretched ahead, stark and rocky. Far too rugged to support even a log cabin. And there was no sign of the rough, wooden dwelling she'd hoped to find.

Katie felt a sense of unreality, as if a dream had morphed into a nightmare. The rain felt wet and cold on her face as she stared at the place where the cabin should have been.

Had it been there once? Had Gabriel moved? Had he taken his prisoner and gone elsewhere?

If so, she would never find him. This was the only link to him, the friendly landlady who had asked about his planned location so long ago, taken an interest, looked at photos, and remembered. If he'd moved again, nobody would ever know where, and perhaps that had been his plan. To disappear completely.

Or perhaps the cabin had been destroyed. A fire, a flood, a lightning strike. Perhaps Gabriel had died. Katie felt the weight of the world on her shoulders as she stared at the empty terrain ahead, where no trace of the building remained.

"Josie. Josie! How could this have happened to you? Why did I think I'd be able to save you?" she whispered.

Tears pricked at her eyes; the disappointment was a crushing weight in her heart. The realization of how close she'd been, how close she'd come to finding her sister, seared her. This was a failure that left her feeling desolate, as if her soul had been torn apart.

Now, she was going to have to go and tell her mother. Katie turned away, feeling devastated, full of grief, uncertain how she was going to break the news.

But as she walked, she felt her fighting spirit start to return. Her crushing grief lifted and in its place, her investigator's brain started second-guessing the situation.

She could have gotten something wrong. She could have misheard, or the landlady might have done so. And logically, nobody would build what had looked like a solid, well-constructed cabin, only to abandon it. That would have been a serious waste of labor and material.

Perhaps she needed to revisit the clues, like a good investigator would do. Recalculate, recalibrate, take a different look at what Mrs. Ingham had said. And then, if she did, she might just find they pointed somewhere else.

But for now, she had to get back to her car, and head to her mother to share this devastating news.

CHAPTER TWO

Three hours later, after a wet, depressing hike back to her car and an endless drive out of the wilderness, Katie pulled up outside her parents' house.

She hadn't wanted to come here now. She felt as if her disappointment was too raw, her emotions too fragile, to deal with them at this moment. If she hadn't promised her mother that she would come by, Katie would have driven straight to the airport.

Sixteen years of estrangement was not something that could be healed in a few days. Not when Katie had been rejected and disowned by her parents, who had blamed her after she'd admitted it had been her idea to go on that reckless kayaking trip, on a river in flood.

Only recently had their relationship started to heal, and Katie had been the one who had made the effort and reached out to her parents again, hoping for their forgiveness, their understanding.

She wasn't sure if they would ever fully repair their relationship, but tentative steps had been made. Her mother had asked Katie to keep her updated on anything she found. She was anxious to know what had happened to her daughter.

But her father felt the opposite. He wanted to wall off that trauma and never think about it again. He didn't want to know, and wouldn't allow it to be mentioned. She and her mother had to keep it a secret from him, that Katie was searching.

Staring at the small, humble home where she'd grown up, outside the tiny town, Katie felt the usual sense of surprise that those four walls, old, solid, and well-made from weathered wood, could have contained so much conflict, so much heartbreak.

She sat for a few moments in the car, staring at the house before her, thinking about the years before Josie's disappearance, the childhood she'd spent here. There had been happy times. But she knew that as soon as she crossed the threshold, all of those memories of togetherness and laughter would be tainted by the shadow of what had happened to Josie, and she would never be able to look back on it the same way.

Katie climbed out of the car and trudged up the short, muddy pathway. She knocked on the door, feeling nervous.

"Katie! You said you'd come by. Is there any news?" Her mother stared at her with worry in her eyes. Her face, always thin, now looked gaunt. The cheerful demeanor Katie remembered was long gone. Time and grief had eroded her spirit, but Katie had the feeling that, although battered, her mother was not quite broken.

"Where's Dad?" Katie asked first, wanting to know if her father was around or not.

"He's asleep. He has a headache. Come through and sit down. You look as if you've been in the rain."

Her mother's keen gaze took in her disheveled and still damp appearance. She led her through to the small lounge. On this rainy day, a fire burned brightly, the flickering flames adding warmth to a room that Katie felt was always chillier than it should be.

"Coffee? Tea?" her mother asked.

"I'm fine, thanks," Katie said. And then, realizing that her mother wanted to bring her something, she said, "Water, please. A glass of water."

Her mother hurried to get it, returning with the glass in a moment. Katie took it, sat down near the fire. She took a thirsty drink of the water.

"Is there any news?" her mother asked in a low voice, sitting opposite. She knew why Katie was here.

Katie hesitated. Her mother was leaning forward, her fingers tapping lightly on her lap. She looked into her mother's eyes, and felt a pang of guilt, knowing that she was going to destroy her hopes.

"Mom, I went looking."

"You went looking? In the place where – where you said you were going to try?" her mother breathed.

"Yes. Mrs. Ingham gave me the approximate area where Gabriel Rath moved to," Katie said.

"You went there?" Her mother stared at her eagerly.

"I've just been to the location where it had to be. But I couldn't find anything there."

"What do you mean?" Her mother frowned.

"I mean, there was no cabin there. No buildings in the woods where there should have been some. She described a cabin, and even showed me a photo he'd sent to her of it half-built. But there was nothing."

"Are you sure you were looking in the right place?"

"I thought I was."

"That's so strange," her mother said, her voice shaking. "It doesn't make sense at all."

"No." Katie gave her a troubled look. "I'm afraid it might have been destroyed. Or Gabriel might have moved again and dismantled it somehow."

"Yes, I guess that must be what happened." Her mother looked crestfallen.

"I wish I'd found something," Katie agreed. "I was sure I was right. But there's also the chance that Mrs. Ingham didn't remember right, or that I made an error, even though I tried hard not to. I'll re-look at it. I'll see if there's anywhere else it could be. But for the time being, it's a dead end. I'm so sorry, Mom."

Her mother wrapped her arms around herself and drew in a shuddering breath. Katie could see the hope in her eyes being extinguished.

"It's not your fault. It was wrong of me to get my hopes up. I shouldn't have."

"No. You shouldn't have." The voice, hard and angry, cut into their low-voiced conversation and Katie spun around, feeling her heart accelerate.

Her father stood at the living room door. His gray hair was tousled, his eyes were reddened, but his expression was furious.

"What is this?" he thundered, turning his gaze from one to the other of them. "What is going on here?"

Katie felt her stomach clench. Their secret was out.

Her dad had heard them talking. Now, he knew that Katie was trying to find out what had happened to Josie, and sharing the information with her mother.

It was a forbidden topic. Her father couldn't handle any mention of her twin.

And clearly, the fact that Katie had been confiding in her mother enraged him. In his eyes, she saw raw pain and betrayal.

"I told you to forget this. To forget it!" he raged, turning to Katie's mother. "This chapter of our life is closed. Opening it will only bring more heartbreak. I've told you again and again. She's gone! Believing otherwise will destroy the both of us!"

Katie, frozen in shock, could only watch as her mother stared up at her father, tears in her eyes.

11

"I was just asking," she said, her voice quivering. "I have a right to ask. If she's still alive, I want to know."

"Josie is dead! She's been dead for sixteen years," her father shouted.

Katie couldn't sit by and watch her mother take the blame for this. She leaped to her feet.

"Dad, I'm the one who's been looking, not Mom. Don't shout at her like that. You can't blame her for trying to find out what happened to Josie."

"There's nothing to find!"

"What if there is?" Katie insisted, feeling appalled by the extent of his rage, but determined to stand her ground.

"You don't have any right to think that way," her dad shouted, his face florid with anger. "You weren't out there, searching for hours and days with the police, until it was clear that there was no trace of her and never will be. Why are you opening the old wounds again? We've put this behind us."

"No, you have not. It's not behind you at all. It's destroying you. Eating away at you. You haven't handled it. I can see it. Can't you?" Katie challenged him.

But he was not ready to listen, especially not to those words, which Katie thought must have hit home too closely.

"What you've done to my wife is unforgivable. Get out! Get out of my house!"

Katie felt her chest tighten with the hurt that his words caused her. She'd made an effort, she'd tried to do what was right, but her father couldn't handle it. His deeply repressed emotion was surging, and now it was expressing itself as anger, directed at her.

"Go, damn you!" he roared.

Her mother, tears running down her cheeks, now joined in the shouting. "Please, stop this," she entreated him. "Katie's my daughter! You can't drive her away; I won't have it. This is my house too, and she's only doing what I asked."

But her father stood his ground, his rage focused on Katie.

"I told you to leave it alone. I told you to forget it all! Is that what you want, to destroy your mother and me, to destroy our life? You do what you like with your life, but I won't let you ruin ours. Get out of my house. I don't want to speak to you again. Don't come back. Do not contact us again."

Katie stared at him, shocked to her core. This was far worse than she'd been expecting. Her father spoke the words with absolute conviction. He meant every hurtful, scorching one. And there was nothing she could do. Staying here was only going to inflame a volatile situation. She needed to leave.

Without a word, Katie stood up.

She walked to the door, stepped through it, and closed it behind her, hearing her mother sobbing brokenly as it shut.

Katie practically staggered back to her car, feeling emotionally flayed. Her legs felt weak, shaky. She couldn't believe what had just played out. The pain. The denial. The anger.

No wonder things between herself and her parents were so strained. The repressed emotions were like poison, toxic and corrosive.

But Katie knew she was not giving up. This confrontation made her even more determined to search for Gabriel Rath.

No matter what it took, she was going to find answers, and get closure, so that she could try to give her parents a way out of the purgatory they were living in.

CHAPTER THREE

Detective Leblanc stepped out of his apartment, which was on the bank of the St. Mary's river that divided the town of Sault Ste. Marie into the U.S. side and the Canadian side. Checking his phone, he felt his heart speed up as he reread the message that had arrived a few minutes earlier.

The message was from Scott, the leader of the cross-border task force that he and Katie worked for.

"We have a new case called in. Murder. On the Minnesota border. The circumstances are bizarre. Come in as soon as you can. Be ready to travel after your briefing."

A new case. That always got Leblanc's blood racing. A detective to his core, he couldn't wait to hear more about what the bizarre circumstances were. Already, he was eager to start the hunt to bring the killer to justice.

It was a cold, rainy Monday morning, but despite the grim weather, he was walking to work. It was only a ten minute walk, and it would be easy to take a cab to the airport. Despite the gray morning, he felt his heart lift as he closed and locked his apartment, slinging his small travel bag over his shoulder. He pulled up the hood of his raincoat, shielding his short, dark hair from the rain as he strode down the street.

He was going to see Katie again. His investigation partner, and now, his lover, too.

Leblanc felt incredibly lucky that he'd had a second chance after losing the love of his life, Celeste, who had worked with him in the Paris police force.

He'd never thought he'd be able to pick up the pieces of his heart, and that he'd be a broken man forever.

In fact, his emotional pain had almost guided him down a destructive path. He'd recently come close to accepting a senior position as the head of the investigation department in central Paris, for all the wrong reasons. He'd wanted the job because part of the new head's responsibility was going to be to decide which prisoners got moved to an older, less well-run facility. One of the prisoners was Hugo Gagnon, Celeste's killer. Leblanc had dreamed of putting his name on the list, moving him to a prison where opposition gangs were in power and where it was very likely he would be murdered.

But Katie had found out his intentions and, with a tongue-lashing he'd never forgotten, had turned him away from that disastrous choice in time. Leblanc felt a huge sense of relief, a weight off his shoulders, that he hadn't been tempted into it.

Swiping rain from his face, Leblanc took a moment to glance at the beautiful architecture of the downtown buildings he was passing, appreciating the Renaissance revival style of this elegant historical area. Part of the reason he loved this town was that it reminded him of Europe.

But he felt a pang as he remembered that their task force was under threat. Their time here might be limited if the powers that be decided to close them down for political reasons. He had heard that might happen, even though the details, and who was behind it, were unknown to him.

Leblanc shook his head, walking faster as if he could get away from these unpleasant thoughts. He could do nothing about that decision. All he could do was his best, working with Katie, keeping their romance a secret so that it did not represent a conflict of interest, and pouring everything he had into the cases.

He reached the door of the old warehouse, newly converted to offices, where the task force operated from. Opening it, he felt glad to be getting inside and out of the cold, drumming rain.

He walked into the warm, stark, functional interior of the building.

There was the fit, lean Scott, his graying hair neatly cut, preparing for the briefing. Scott was setting up a laptop, connecting it to a video screen, with a tray of coffee already waiting on the small kitchenette table.

"Good morning," he greeted his boss.

"Morning, Leblanc," Scott replied.

Then, quick, light footsteps came through from the boardroom. His heart clenched as he saw Katie. Her shiny brown hair, her green eyes.

"Hey, Leblanc," she said, with a quick smile.

Last night, she'd come around to his place, and he'd held her, wiping her tears away as he'd listened to the heart-rending account of her search for Gabriel Rath, and how her father had disowned her once again. He'd banned her from the house, even going so far as to block her phone number so she could no longer call her parents.

He'd stroked her brown hair, listened, until he'd seen the fighting spirit come back into her eyes and knew that she was over the worst of her intense grief.

But at work they would not mention what had happened between them in private.

"Morning, Katie," he said. "I can't wait to hear more about the case."

"Let me brief you now," Scott said, his preparations complete.

Seeing they were a small task force, they seldom all worked on the same cases. Scott coordinated events from this central hub, and Leblanc and Katie worked as a pair, as did Clark and Anderson. Johnson, the police psychologist, assisted either in his research capacity or as an additional team member, and his analytical skills were invaluable.

So for today, Leblanc was not surprised that it was only him and Katie in the office, and that the others were deployed elsewhere.

"Sit down," Scott invited them.

Leblanc poured coffee for everyone as Scott got the details up onto the big screen.

"We have a very strange and disturbing set of circumstances here," he said. "So far, two female victims have been found near a construction site on the northern Minnesota border. They have been strangled, and then carried up tall trees where they have been wedged."

"What?" Leblanc exclaimed. He saw Katie's eyes narrow in surprise at this shocking scenario.

"The first woman, Nikita Walton, age thirty, was found three days ago. Hikers on the Minnesota side of the border saw her body up in a tree about a mile from the site. They called police immediately. When her body was identified, the local police connected with the RCMP, and confirmed that she was a Canadian local who lived about two miles from the border, and must have been jogging in the forest at the time she was killed. She shared a house with two friends who confirmed her early morning running routine. It seems likely that she strayed unintentionally across the border during her run. Cause of death was confirmed as strangulation."

"And the next one?" Katie asked. Leblanc could see she was utterly focused on the circumstances of each kill.

"That was late yesterday afternoon. Again, the victim was found high up in a tree, a few hundred yards from where forest clearing is taking place. Two local kids found the body. The woman, Clarissa Hughes, age thirty-five, actually works for the construction operation.

She's a land surveyor. She'd worked until dark the previous day, and had been reported missing at breakfast time. Nobody thought to search the treetops. Until she was found, the police had no idea they were dealing with a serial killer. When they did realize, they called me first thing this morning. Apparently she liked to go for early walks in the forest before work, and they are guessing that is when she was taken."

Leblanc exchanged a glance with Katie.

"Anything in common between the victims, at a glance?" It was important to rule this out, even though proximity to the construction site seemed to be the most obvious common factor.

"No. Nothing in common. One was a Canadian local and the other was on site for the operation, and actually lives in Maine. They're not connected in any obvious way."

Leblanc looked at the map of the area that Scott was displaying on the screen. The sites were very close to each other, and both were close to the construction site.

Leblanc knew it was too early to see a pattern, and that jumping to conclusions would be unwise, but he could already see a way forward, the first steps they would need to take with this case.

"You're booked on a flight to Falls International Airport in a couple of hours," Scott said. "From there, a rental car is reserved. At the site, the local police department will meet you and work with you on the case. I've sent through all the reports so far. Do you have any questions?"

Leblanc felt Katie tense, and take a decisive breath.

"I'm happy with the information we have so far on the case. It's very thorough as always, Scott. But I'd like to know what's happening with our task force. I've been hearing rumors. I'd like to get the truth. Are we going to be closed down?"

Leblanc didn't like what he saw in Scott's face as Katie asked that difficult question. He didn't like it at all. He waited, feeling as anxious as Katie looked, to see what his answer was going to be.

CHAPTER FOUR

Katie watched Scott carefully as he prepared to speak. She could see that there were things he didn't want to tell them. He was frowning, thinking.

After a pause, he said, "Yes, I'd not be honest with you if I said everything was okay."

"What is it?" she pressured him. "Why is this happening?"

He grimaced. "Politics. One of the state governors has influenced others. I can't say more. But I will say this." He stared at them both, looking as serious as she'd ever seen him. "I believe in this task force. I believe that you are both outstanding investigators, as are the other three team members. Our results have been beyond criticism. We've had a phenomenal solve rate. I believe that what we are doing here is vitally important, not just for the police on both sides of the border, targeting the specialized crimes that they don't have capacity for, but for society as a whole. We have helped a traditionally dangerous and difficult area become safer."

"I agree," Katie said. But her heart was racing and she felt a knot of worry tighten in her stomach. She wanted to ask, how long? How long before we're shut down? How long before I have to leave Leblanc and leave this task force?

But that was selfish, and she knew she needed to hold it together as Scott continued.

"What I believe in even more strongly is the integrity of you both. I think you are the best crime-fighting duo I have ever worked with. I want to see you continue with this operation. I'm going to do whatever I can to ensure that the task force continues in its current format, with its current scope and powers."

"Thank you," Leblanc said, standing up and shaking Scott's hand. "We appreciate you fighting for us."

"Politics has been our enemy before. It can be fought. Not always, but sometimes," Scott acknowledged.

Katie stood, too, picking up her travel bag. "If there's anything I can do, please tell me. And meanwhile, we'd better get to the airport."

Scott pressed keys on his phone. "Your cab should be outside in five minutes."

"Let's go and wait," Katie said. She headed outside to the covered porch, to wait for the cab, feeling uncharacteristically unsure.

"I don't want anything to happen with us. Not now," she said to Leblanc in a low voice.

They were at work, so she didn't even dare to take his hand. In working hours, they were colleagues. Only after work were they lovers. But she knew, from the grim nod of acknowledgement he gave, that he understood the bleakness of the scenario.

"Where would you go?" she asked him.

"Not back to Paris," he said immediately. She felt relieved about that as he continued. "I gave it some thought, wondering what I would do if the worst happened. But I feel that time of my life is past. A new department head has been appointed. He'll be making the decisions. It's not my home anymore. I've moved on." His voice was hard.

Including the decision about whether to transfer his partner's killer to the less secure prison. That would now fall onto the new incumbent's shoulders and it might be happening soon, if she recalled the timeline correctly. Katie could see that Leblanc hadn't completely let go of the issue. There was something in his eyes that told her he was still following that outcome. That he still wanted to know Gagnon's fate.

"I want to be somewhere I can still see you," he then blurted out. "Europe is not that place."

Katie shook her head. "I'm FBI. I have to go where I'm deployed. If the task force is disbanded, that could be anywhere in the States. It might not be back to the unit where I was working previously, and it might not be close to the border at all."

"I suppose we could make it work long distance," he said.

"It seldom works long distance," Katie said. "That's not what I want. I'll take it if I have to, if it means a hope of us staying together, but the best case is that this unit remains, that we get a guarantee of its longevity, that this struggle for petty power leaves us alone."

"Agreed," Leblanc said.

Staring out at the rain, Katie felt for a moment that their future may be as bleak as the weather.

"There's our cab," she said, relieved to be able to climb inside and focus on moving forward, getting to the crime scene, and solving the case that challenged them now. She knew how important this was, not only to get a dangerous killer out of circulation, but because a success at this time might just make a difference to the unit's fight for survival.

*

Three hours later, Katie and Leblanc climbed out of the rental SUV that had taken them on the last leg of their journey, deep into the woods, along the rutted road that led into the area close to the small town of Ashton, where the forest was being cleared.

Their first stop was going to be the construction site. As they pulled up outside the site entrance, Katie was surprised by how large the development was. It looked as if, so far, about a hundred acres of forest had been cleared, and from the crews at work on the forest borders, it seemed more was planned. She climbed out of the car at the site entrance, where a temporary boom had been set up on the newly constructed dirt road leading into the site.

Immediately, the noise hit her. She was used to the quiet of the woods. Now, the shrieking of saws, the growling of machinery, the repetitive beeping of excavators at work, filled the air. A faint dust seemed to hang above the newly cleared area, which looked like a big scar in the otherwise lush forest. There were a host of vehicles parked inside the boom, some with construction equipment attached.

An attendant hurried over to meet them. The young, gangly man wore a yellow safety jacket and a white hard hat.

"Good morning. Can I help?"

"We're investigators, here to follow up on the crimes."

"The crimes. Thanks for coming here to help out," the young man said earnestly. "Do you want to meet with the police on site? One of them is here now."

"That sounds good," Katie said.

The man indicated a box by the gate.

"Please, can you put on hard hats? Everyone on site has to wear them. It's a safety regulation."

"Sure," Katie said.

She took a white hat out of the box and fastened it securely on her head. Leblanc did the same.

The young attendant got on his walkie-talkie and spoke into it rapidly.

"The police detective on site is Detective Sheldon. He'll be here in a minute."

It was only half a minute later before a stressed-looking police detective, wearing a heavy jacket and a hard-hat, arrived. He looked to be in his forties, and Katie guessed from his flushed, chubby face that his job had recently kept him behind a desk, not walking miles out in the forest.

"Agent Winter and Detective Leblanc," Katie introduced their team.

"It's good to meet you," Sheldon said. "This is a very puzzling crime scene, and it's as clean as I've ever seen. I've been searching for any trace evidence, any clues, while I waited for you to arrive. I haven't found anything, but in the meantime, would you like to see the most recent place where they found the surveyor's body? Perhaps seeing the site will be helpful? And then, if you like, I can take you to interview the witness who found her. He is a young man who lives locally, in the town a mile away."

"Let's start with the scene of the crime," Katie said.

She knew this was going to be important. The crime scene was going to give them a bigger picture, more details, as well as the feel of what had played out. She could feel her pulse quicken in anticipation.

Katie hoped that the physical site would give her some insight about his modus operandi and his thought processes that she hadn't yet gained from the written reports. With such a bizarre scenario created for his kills, Katie knew she would need all the clues into his thinking that she could get.

CHAPTER FIVE

Scott sat at his desk, alone in the task force office. He barely noticed the rain lashing at the windows, as he confronted the serious problem of the task force's survival.

The situation was precarious.

He had to tread very carefully, dealing with the highly influential governor in Washington. Politically ambitious, and seeing the task force as a threat to his power, this man was determined to prove it to be a waste of money and disband it. He'd gained the support of governors in no less than three other states along the border, including Minnesota, where Katie and Leblanc were now headed. It was creating a groundswell of resistance to the work of the task force.

But Scott knew what a knife-edge politics could be. He had to ensure that he spoke to people in such a way that they wanted to help, and didn't feel threatened into taking action against him.

It was more serious than he'd told Katie and Leblanc. He knew that both of them, perceptive as they were, had realized he wasn't saying everything he knew.

He'd been sent the minutes of a high-level meeting, where FBI, RCMP, police chiefs and other players had convened. The task force had supporters, particularly within the RCMP, and Scott also thought that the FBI had been on their side. But the counter-arguments were persuasive. One of the main drawbacks they faced was that the task force was so new.

The governor who wanted it disbanded, a man that Scott was wary of because he was staying in the background and pulling strings, was calling the successes coincidental. He'd been making this claim for a while now.

Cynically, Scott wondered how many successes were required before this word stopped being used.

But the task force could not afford any detractors, because it was so new. It needed the support of the people who were currently making decisions, and Scott knew time was running out.

In despair, he stared at the rows of case files on the shelf opposite his desk. The records of success. Every case showed the courage and tenacity of the seasoned investigation professionals that he felt humbled to work with every day.

These individuals were driven, passionate and talented, and they saved lives. Scott was proud to serve with them. And he was determined that their work had to continue.

He couldn't let it end. He felt a deep responsibility to ensure these files, these achievements were not lost to an uncaring world. At the same time, he knew that they couldn't continue without the political backing they needed.

Inside the files were the names of all the victims. Lists of names that haunted Scott. His only comfort was that these lists were not any longer, and that was thanks to the speed and determination of his team in tackling these often difficult cases. With their strategic brilliance, their skills, their knowledge of the area, they were able to target the criminals before more deaths had occurred.

The task force had so much going for it. The FBI was working well with it. They had good working relationships with the RCMP and their Canadian counterparts, and they had a lot of support from local police, who were in turn very positive about the added manpower and the extra level of expertise they provided.

They had a strong team in place and they had proven themselves.

But negativity was infectious. One persuasive individual who was against something could spread the sentiment to suit him. Using the age-old arguments that always seemed to gain ground.

Costs. The unit was doubling up on costs. The agents were expensive. They were not on low pay grades. In the northern areas, resources were scarce and using them was expensive, too.

And there were always those ambitious individuals within the police who would jump on the bandwagon to claim they could do a better job and that the unit was treading on their turf, preventing them from doing their work correctly.

Scott knew he had to think of a way to turn the tide so that the few could not sway the views of the many.

And he had to do it fast. It was time for him to play one of his last cards. His only remaining card.

There was a retired FBI agent who had occupied an extremely senior position in the department. He had since gone into the political world, and was both influential and a man of integrity. Scott respected him immensely.

Furthermore, he was Katie Winter's mentor and had worked with her closely when she had first joined the FBI.

His name was Agent Timms.

Years before, Scott had worked with him on a cooperative, joint venture between the U.S. and Canadian policing, so there was a personal connection there.

Scott picked up the phone and dialed Timms's private cellphone number.

"Detective Scott?" he answered in three rings, sounding surprised.

"Agent Timms. Thanks for taking my call. I would only trouble you on your personal cell if it was urgent. This is urgent."

"Tell me the circumstances," he said.

Scott took a deep breath.

"For the past few months, I've headed up the new cross-border task force. It's a joint venture crime-fighting initiative between the USA and Canada."

"I've heard of that. Isn't Katie Winter part of it?" he asked, with a new tone of interest in his voice.

"She's an integral part of it, yes. It's been very successful, but it is coming under pressure from some state politicians who are trying to shut us down."

"Anyone in particular?"

He listened as Scott named the person who he had identified as the one behind the initiative to shut the unit down. This extremely influential and persuasive person was gradually building the groundswell of support to get the unit annihilated.

"I can see why you called me in," Timms said in a less friendly tone.

Scott said nothing, but pressed his lips together anxiously. He hoped that his own relationship with Timms, together with his strong connection to Katie, would outweigh the other factors.

Because the governor looking to close the unit down was a long-standing personal friend of Timms. Loyalties went both ways.

Scott dug his nails into his palm as he waited for feedback. He could have killed the unit by doing this. But he knew it was his only chance. This was the only individual that could change the governor's mind.

Timms finally spoke again. "I'll get back to you when I've thought this through."

Scott waited for more.

When Timms didn't offer more, Scott drew a breath and said, "Thank you, Agent Timms. I appreciate that."

"I don't want to be forced into a position where I have to pick sides. I understand the situation. I'll let you know what I can do, if anything," Timms said curtly, and then hung up.

Scott put the phone down. He stared into space, his thoughts chaotic, his pulse pounding. He had no idea whether Timms's influence would be enough to get the governor to change his mind.

If he gave his support, Timms would not go back on his word. But he had also told Scott that he wouldn't take sides in this matter.

But he didn't know if Timms was going to be willing to do it, or whether he was going to leave it be, not wanting to damage the friendship.

The knife edge hadn't gone away. If anything, it was even more of a delicate balance than it had been.

Tomorrow felt like a lifetime away, and Scott had no idea what the outcome would be.

CHAPTER SIX

Katie couldn't believe what she saw, as she stared up at the starkly impossible scene where the second, more recent, victim had been found. In the background, a couple of hundred yards away, the drone of machinery and clatter of metal still felt disturbing and intrusive to her. The sound made it feel as if the area was under threat. As if all trees were due to fall under this implacable process of annihilation.

But this tree was still standing, and Katie wondered if the development would even reach this far as the clearing operation didn't seem to be touching this area of the forest. This was a massively tall sugar maple, mature, with a thick trunk.

And far up, where the branches split and proliferated into the tree's leafy crown - there, the victim had been found?

She felt perplexed by this. How had she been taken up there? Katie doubted the logistics of using a ladder. This was too high for all but the tallest ladders, and those would surely be under strict control at this construction site, and difficult to move.

Her boggled mind was battling to accept that this body must have been taken up by hand.

The woman was slim and small. Reading the report, Katie had noted that she had been just five-three, slender, light. But even so. The whole way up? Had she been alive at the time? Dead? Tied up?

Katie had so many questions. She saw her own confusion reflected in Leblanc's eyes.

"How is this possible?" he murmured.

Katie had hoped that she'd be able to get an insight into the killer's mind, staring up at this dizzyingly high climb. But all she was getting was a feeling that this man - she was guessing it was a man - was driven by factors that were not understood easily, if at all.

"Was there any trace evidence, whatsoever?" she asked Sheldon.

He shook his head. "Unfortunately not. There had been recent rains. Early that morning, in fact. And then the two boys who discovered the body left their footprints in the soil. We looked, we photographed, but we could find nothing. Even far up. With the rain, the wind, the sheer complexity of the scene. And yet, simplicity," he added thoughtfully.

26

"The first scene, a mile and a half west of here, was identical, except that the hikers who found the body never went up the tree. The victim had been wearing a bright pink jacket, and one of them saw it up in the branches, looked more closely, and called police."

"Were the hikers interviewed?"

"Yes, we interviewed them and asked them if they had seen anyone at all nearby. They didn't see anyone. Unfortunately, the group – a husband, wife, and their seventeen year old daughter – were here on vacation and they flew home to Arizona yesterday. So they are not available for any further questioning, except via phone."

Katie's mind was still reeling.

That impossible, stomach-twisting climb. With a body, leaving it there. Why? How?

"It's bizarre," she said.

"We've checked as much as we can," the officer said apologetically. "Interviewed a few of Clarissa Hughes's colleagues on site. There's not much to find."

"Why's that?" Katie asked.

"She was a replacement. Flown out a couple of weeks ago to stand in for someone who got pneumonia and had to go home. She was relatively new on site and she was only going to be there a few weeks, until the original surveyor was well again. She wasn't part of an established team, and from what we have heard, she got on well with everyone. She did her job quietly. She kept to herself otherwise."

"That definitely seems to rule out a personal motive. And in any case there was another victim," Katie reiterated.

The earlier victim had no connection with anyone on site and had simply strayed into the area near the site while out running. That meant there would be limited use in exploring personal motives.

Instead, they would need to explore suspects. But before she started, Katie wanted to get as much eyewitness detail as she could.

There was a chance that the witness who had found the body might possibly have seen or remembered something. Even the tiniest detail could help. She knew how it was. Sometimes, in shock, things were forgotten that were remembered later.

And there was always a chance the killer had been in the area, hiding away, waiting to see the shock value of his work. Perhaps the boys who'd found the body had glimpsed him, and might remember something now.

"Where is the witness?" she asked. "Can we go into town now? You said it was close by?"

"Sure. From here, the town is very close by. It's literally a five minute drive. I'll take you in my car and then bring you back."

Katie hurried behind him to the police SUV that was parked among the medley of vehicles at the entrance. She felt encouraged to be making a start. She was always hopeful that the first testimonies might provide a guiding point.

They climbed into the car and set off for the town. The town was so small that Katie hadn't even seen the tarred access road, a narrow blacktop strip among the trees, leading through the forest.

When the trees cleared a mile or two further on, she saw it was a surprisingly pretty town, nestled against a backdrop of hills and woods, with ski slopes among the trees. It was comprised of a few rows of houses with a little strip of shops and restaurants, and a couple of hotels and motels.

"What is the forest being cleared for? Do you know?" she asked.

Sheldon nodded. "Government planning. The town is called Ashton. For years, they have wanted to create a North Ashton, with space for more houses, a high school, a sports center, a conference center, and a few more facilities to encourage tourism. They've finally got the permissions for it. It's a positive thing, actually. Unlike many small towns, this one is growing and thriving thanks to its location near the border, and the increasing demand for tourism. I've seen the plans. Unfortunately, some forest does have to be cleared, but it's been planned with minimum impact on the environment, and it's going to be a great long term prospect. It's why these murders are especially disturbing."

"That's interesting," Katie said. She hadn't realized that it was a positive and planned addition to the scenic town, and Sheldon was right. It added to the negative impact of this murder. The state would have invested a lot in this, and she was sure that they would already be pressuring Scott for results.

With a flash of fear, she remembered that the fate of the unit might hang in the balance. At this time, failure might mean more than just an unsolved case.

"Here we are." Sheldon parked the car and they got out.

Katie breathed in fresh air that was cool and fragrant after the morning rains. Sheldon had stopped outside a small wooden cottage. It was set in a tiny but well tended yard, and backed onto the forest, which felt like a solid, dark green shield behind it.

She followed him up to the house. The door was opened before Sheldon even lifted his hand to the bell.

An anxious looking woman in her early forties, with a pleasant, weathered face stood there.

"You want to speak to Gavin?" she asked. "He's inside."

"How's he feeling?" Sheldon asked her considerately, reminding Katie all over again about the difference in relationships within a small town. The police were personal friends and mentors within such a small community, which she thought was the way it should be.

"He's better now. Over his shock. He's spoken to a few friends. His aunt and cousins are arriving later, and we have a family dinner planned which we hope will cheer him up. But come in."

They stepped inside, through the postage-stamp size hall, and into the kitchen that was clearly the center of the home. A fire burned in the corner. Gavin, a tall, athletic looking teenager with his mother's anxious expression, sat at the table.

"Hi, Gavin. We've got a few more police here, to ask you questions. Agent Winter and Detective Leblanc are helping with the investigation," Sheldon said heartily.

Gavin jumped to his feet, looking startled. "Good – good morning," he stammered.

"Sit, please." Katie perched on a chair herself. "It must have been a big shock."

"It was," Gavin acknowledged, lowering himself back down.

"What happened?" Katie asked.

"My friend Mike and I were on a dare," Gavin said, sounding reluctant to have to repeat the facts of his misdemeanor.

"What kind of dare?" Leblanc asked him.

"Who could climb higher. We do it every so often. I mean, it's dangerous but fun."

Katie nodded understanding.

"We chose the tallest tree around. I think Mike picked it this time."

"Because you could go higher?"

"Exactly. But it wasn't an easy climb. When I got near the top I started slipping. I got scared. I reached out to try and grab at something and I - I caught her arm. I pulled it down. It was just, like, unreal. Her face was in front of me, I was looking into her eyes. I nearly fell. I was yelling, screaming. Mike had hold of my leg. He managed to help me down to a lower branch. Then, somehow, we got down again, but I don't remember that part so well." He shook his head, as if shaking the terrifying memories away.

"So she was concealed in the tree?"

He nodded. "Totally. We didn't see a thing when we looked up."

"Was that part of the forest familiar to you?"

"Sort of. But we hadn't been there yet this year. Not since winter."

"Did you see anyone else around when you were there?"

He shook his head. "No. I know that for a fact, because we looked. You see, were worried we might get into trouble for the climbing, especially because it was quite close to that site and there were warning notices everywhere. *Don't go closer, trespassers will be prosecuted, heavy machinery at work, beware of starting fires close to a construction site.* That sort of thing. So we did look carefully. There was definitely no-one else around."

"What did you feel when you saw her as you were climbing?" Katie asked. Since she was getting no real information from a witness perspective, she wondered if she might pick something up from his impressions at the time.

"It was so weird. It was like, she shouldn't have been there," Gavin said thoughtfully. "It almost felt like she must have been dropped from the sky. I mean, that was my first thought. That she'd been dropped, like a bird of prey had taken her."

Katie nodded somberly.

For sure, a predator had done these kills. Only they were dealing with an evil, damaged human being, rather than a bird of prey, acting on instinct.

And now, they had to find him, with only the barest trail of evidence to lead them there. But there was an important thread in common and that was the presence of the site itself. A site that had brought together workers from far and wide. Among the many teams of people who'd invaded this quiet rural area, a criminal might be lurking.

She knew what her next step was going to be. Katie wanted to speak to the construction site manager, and see if he had noticed anything unusual or troubling in his operation, or his workers' behavior, over the past few days.

CHAPTER SEVEN

"Where can we find the site manager?" Katie asked Sheldon. This was going to be an important interview. The sooner they got to it, the better.

Sheldon shrugged. "He's a very busy man and he moves around on site all the time. I have spoken to him once. He's very worried about this, but at the same time, he's in a rush to finish the job and keep it on schedule. His name's Al Carver. I'll contact the gate guards and ask them where he's likely to be."

He picked up the phone, and dialed a number. His voice was so low that Katie couldn't make out the words, but she could hear the urgency of his tone.

"They say you can find him at the main construction office. For the next ten minutes, at least. I'll take you there."

Katie felt hopeful about the insight this person could bring. She was sure that if the killer was someone who was involved in the project, this would be an important first step to tracking him down.

They headed back out of town, along the raw, earth track. This time, Sheldon led them a different way. As soon as they were through the main gates, he turned sharply right, following a winding track up the hill.

The clouds were dissipating, and glimpses of blue sky flickered through the surrounding pines.

They entered a clearing, where a bulldozer was already at work, churning the earth. With a massive grinding, shrieking sound as soil was dug and rocks were moved, it was creating an even broader clearing for the construction to take place. It looked ready to start the next section of the site, maybe thirty feet away.

On the edge of the clearing, a converted container was doing duty as an office.

"It's pretty busy in there, so I'll ask him to come out," Sheldon advised, before hurrying inside. A few moments later, he came out, followed by a tall, strongly built man, with a lined, tanned face. Katie guessed him to be in his late forties. He had a calm, businesslike demeanor. He was wearing a hard hat, jeans, and a plaid shirt.

31

"Al Carver?" she asked.

"That's me," he replied. He stared at them unsmilingly, but she didn't pick up any animosity. She sensed this was a man who wanted to get things done as fast as possible, and with minimal fuss along the way.

"Agent Winter and Detective Leblanc," Katie introduced them. "We need to get some background on the situation here."

Carver made a face. "Look, it's an enormous site, and the phases of construction are following on from each other to save on time. We have about a hundred people working full time here at the moment, and of those, about half are living on site, and the rest are residing in town. Then in addition to that, we have, at any given time, up to fifty contractors from elsewhere on site."

Katie raised her eyebrows. Those were bigger numbers than she'd expected.

"It's a multi-phase project," Carver reiterated. "Clearing the forest, and then going straight on to construct the layout, the roads, and put in the structures. We have a short summer season here where it's easy and more affordable to build, so we're looking to use our time as best we can."

"With so many people on site, have you noticed any fights? Any troublemakers? Conflict that might have led to this?"

Carver shook his head. "I personally have not, and I have been looking out for any problems. I run a very tight ship. My managers all have to account for any slip-ups, and I mean anything. Broken equipment, missing machinery, any interpersonal conflict, any absenteeism. They report daily to me on these and I check and action the reports daily. We have health and safety inspections. We have precautions in place for injury, floods, and fire. The local forest fire watch is going to be monitoring the site in a couple of weeks' time."

Katie believed him. He spoke with conviction, and she got the sense he was a competent person, experienced, and on top of his game. And the site reflected it. It was neat, efficient, and looked organized despite its massive size and complexity.

"Any criminal records among the crew?" Leblanc asked.

He shook his head. "We background check all our employees and I hire nobody who has a criminal record. However, I must admit, that we can't check the personnel hired by all the contractors we employ. We simply don't have time for that. So yes, there is a chance that one of our contractors could have hired someone with a criminal record, on a temporary basis, to help with this workload." He sighed. "Some things are not within our control."

That, to Katie, represented the best starting point for them to explore.

"I have two favors I would like to ask of you," she said.

"What are those? I'll action them straight away," Carver said.

"The first is to put the word out that we're here. If any worker has concerns, they are welcome to approach us in confidence or else give us a call. We will treat all information with the strictest confidence. But someone might know something and if so, we need to open the doors for them to talk."

"I'll do that within the hour," Carver promised. "I'll message all our workers, and send the same message out to the subcontractors to tell their staff. What's the second favor?"

"We are going to need to go out and interview your contractors. Would you be able to give us a list of which outside contractors are on site today, and where they are working? And if there are any who were here yesterday, but who have left or completed their job?"

"Sure. I'll need a few minutes to compile it for you. I'll do it as fast as possible," he said. "We haven't had any contractors leave since yesterday. Everyone who's working today, worked yesterday too."

"Thank you," Katie said.

He turned and hurried back into the office. Through one of the small windows, she saw the space inside was small and crowded and frantically busy. It might be early days on the construction site, but the clock was already ticking down to a deadline.

At that moment, Sheldon rushed over.

"There's some new information that's just come in," he said. "We've received the coroner's report. He's a very good pathologist who works here in Minnesota. Although the first victim had her postmortem completed on the Canadian side of the border, they made the results available to him. So he has detailed information on both the victims."

Katie looked at Leblanc, feeling hopeful. This might bring them something new in terms of evidence.

"Where is he based?" she asked Sheldon. "Can we meet with him?"

"Unfortunately, the pathology unit where he works is nearly a hundred miles from here. Distances, you know," he said regretfully.

Katie weighed up her options. A hundred miles was a long drive, especially since Carver was busy compiling a report that would be ready in a few minutes, and which they would need to check out same-day.

She decided that they could not afford the time it would take to drive there and speak to this pathologist personally. Not when there was so much to do on site, in such a changing landscape.

"Let's call him," she decided.

"Here's his number," Sheldon said, with a nod of agreement that this was the best solution. "His name is Dr. Ivans."

Katie walked over to the tree line to make the call, getting as far as she could from the persistent noise that her brain was now beginning to tune out.

"Can I speak to Dr. Ivans?" she asked. "It's FBI Agent Winter calling, in connection with the reports on the murder victims from the forest."

Katie hoped this quick introduction would open doors faster, and so it did.

"Hold on a moment, I'll get him on the line for you," the receptionist said. In a few beats, Katie was speaking to a deep-voiced man.

"Dr. Ivans here."

"Dr. Ivans, it's Agent Winter. I'm calling to speak to you about the postmortems on the two murder victims from the Ashton area. Could you share your findings over the phone?"

Katie retreated even further into the cover of the trees, as a new rattling from the construction site began. Leblanc walked with her, leaning over to hear the conversation, which Katie had at full volume.

"Of course I can. I've examined the second victim, and also read through the report from the first victim," Dr. Ivans said in measured tones.

"What are your conclusions?" Katie asked.

"Undoubtedly, the cause of death is the same for both victims. Strangulation in both instances. Efficiently done, from behind, by a right handed individual. The bodies were both found clothed, and there was no sign of a struggle. No defensive wounds, but the cut and scrape marks on the faces and hands would indicate that they were carried up the trees."

"So they would have been overpowered immediately, at ground level, and then the bodies carried up?" Katie confirmed.

"Yes. Strange as it sounds, I think that's what happened. The strangulation would have been quick, there is no evidence of any other injury such as a head injury, nothing untoward in the toxicology reports, so that's the only scenario that makes sense."

"How tall were they? Any common factors?" Katie was wondering how strong this killer would have had to be.

"They were both petite women. Five-two and five-four, slim builds. Apart from that they are not similar looking. The first victim is dark haired, the second victim is blonde. They are five years apart in age."

Katie nodded. So apart from choosing individuals that were smaller in build, it did not appear so far that this killer was targeting a particular type of woman.

"How were they secured in the trees?"

"They were literally wrapped around a branch. It seems like this killer must have arranged them there while dead. Neither of them were secured at all, they were just nestled into a crook of the branch."

"That's just bizarre." Shaking her head, Katie met Leblanc's gaze.

"I know. I've never seen anything like it before. It would have taken nerve, strength, and skill."

"Any other evidence, any indications, any traces left behind?" Katie asked hopefully.

"I wish I could give you more. Both the scenes were very clean. There's nothing on the bodies that can tell me more," Ivans said regretfully. "I don't know what you're dealing with. Someone strong, someone reasonably light, and someone who sure is a dangerous individual," he said somberly.

"Thank you for your help," Katie said.

She cut the call. This had been disappointing. They hadn't gained the insight she'd hoped for. Beyond knowing they were looking for a strong, fairly light, athletic, and right-handed man.

At that moment, Carver rushed out of the construction office, holding a sheaf of printed pages.

"Agents, I have the list you need," he called.

Eagerly, Katie hurried over. It was time to go out and see if the boots-on-the-ground approach might narrow down who this killer was, and if he was hiding among the hordes of contractors at this site.

CHAPTER EIGHT

Eagle was perched in a tree, high above the grinding bustle of the machinery and the activity of the site. He felt far removed from it. Physically and mentally, too. He was not among the people toiling below, with their bulldozers and chainsaws. He was above them.

He liked heights; he always had. He'd always felt at home in high places. At first he'd felt safe, as if he was in a secure hideaway. But then, slowly, that feeling had changed.

Now, he didn't feel safe, so much as powerful.

Being far above ground level gave him a deep, inherent sense of power. It was the only time he felt it, because at all other times he lacked it. He felt futile, damaged, not good enough.

At least he was alone here, alone with his thoughts, able to watch, and to be an observer of what was taking place.

Looking down, Eagle could see the endless back and forth of the yellow machines. Tracking to and fro, guzzling the trees, leaving blackened soil and splintered stumps behind. The splintering crashes as trees were felled. It was chaos down there at ground level. Grinding, splintering chaos.

But up here, it was quieter. In this high canopy, hidden from view, he felt as if he could breathe. He could hear the rustling of the leaves, the sighing of the wind that made that strange restlessness surge inside him. It was an odd feeling, a feeling of imbalance. That he didn't belong here.

He was not meant to be here, down on the rocky, muddy earth. That was not where he wanted to be, or where he felt his heart was. He never had.

He needed to go higher, go further, go outside of himself. He needed to become more.

Looking up, he watched a bird of prey, soaring above him, and felt the deep connection intensify.

Those powerful wings, taking him high. Seeing the world from the air, looking down at the swathes of forest, the tracts of mountain, the flat, checkerboard farming plains. The sea and the lakes.

He wanted to be above them all.

Going higher was his only direction. How he envied that bird, with its effortless flight. It would be so much richer, more rewarding, if he could be a bird.

He felt the yearning to launch himself, to take flight, to follow the soaring bird. To soar, to turn. To spiral, to dive.

He reached out a hand to touch the branch he was balanced on, and closed his eyes. He could see the bird in his mind, feel it flying, feel the wind of its flight.

He felt the restless energy shift inside him, awaken and quicken. Swooping in for the kill.

That was his dream, his obsession. It was what he wanted to become.

He watched the bird circling, high above. It was an eagle, he thought. Floating on the thermals in the warming air. Gliding in the dizzying heights. What would the forest look like from up there?

What would it look like from that height, from that perspective?

In the eagle's eyes, he was assessing the stumps of the recently fallen trees, where the forest had been shorn of its greatest trees, and the earth had been torn up by the roots. Perhaps small creatures were scurrying away, representing prey.

He was scoping out the splintered stumps, and the darkening ground. He was looking at the destruction that had been wrought upon the forest.

He could hear it all: the grinding of their progress, the splintering of the trees, the crashing of their fall.

He saw their work and their strength. He understood their inexorable power.

But it meant nothing to him, not from where he flew. Because he would be more powerful.

From his airborne vantage point, he acknowledged the many varied faces of the machines, their shapes tiny from this height, their noises distant. Because from up there, so high, he was the master of his world, and anything in it.

Being a predator came with power, and he needed to use that power to complete himself. It was time to continue his work. He rose, and felt as if he stretched his own wings. He would become like the birds. He could, he knew it.

The eagle soared above him, gliding on the thermals. He felt the connection shift, close in on him. All at once, he felt at one with the bird, ready to glide in for the kill. He had to swoop in, high above the trees.

He needed to be that bird, that eagle. He had to soar.

The bird wheeled. Then, like a masterful diver, it swooped out of its spiral, plummeting down. He closed his eyes, and felt himself swooping down too.

He felt the air rush past his head, and opened his eyes.

And found himself looking into the sightless gaze of his recent prey. He let out a breathy sigh at the memory.

He'd taken her soundlessly. She hadn't known a thing. The kill had been quick, savage, and efficient. As he had done it, he had felt like a bird of prey swooping onto a tiny, helpless animal. Quickly, with claw-like hands, he had dispatched the woman. It had been even faster than his first kill, more lethal. It showed him that his efforts were being rewarded and that he could one day become what he dreamed of.

It had felt good. The first time had been good, the second time, better.

Just as a young bird of prey needed to learn to kill, so Eagle was learning, too.

And then, after the kill, feeling the pull of the high branches drawing him there, he had taken her where he needed to.

Up to the trees. The circle was complete.

In his mind, Eagle felt a shift. He was closer to his goal now; he knew that without a doubt.

How many more kills would be needed? He didn't know. But he knew that with each one, he would have to be more careful and more cunning.

Just as a predator needed to escape his own enemies, so he knew he would have to escape detection by people who didn't understand his need. Not everyone would accept this had to happen, even though it was necessary, and he knew it was a part of nature. Even in this place where nature was getting destroyed to make way for humanity.

They would be hiding away now, in fear. Trying to shelter, away from his reach, but they did not know how far he could reach. And how carefully he had thought about his goals.

The next time must be soon, he couldn't leave it too long, because the transformation needed to happen. He didn't know how it would happen, but he felt sure it would. He just had to follow his instincts.

His instincts would draw him to the weaker prey. He had an idea in mind, and earlier he'd glimpsed a few who might be suitable for his next catch.

He couldn't wait to carry it out. To kill again. To stalk, to fall on his prey, cruel and fast.

What would he do differently this time? The kill would be even more efficient, that he knew. The hesitancy was gone now. This time he would be cruelly confident. And he was learning to be more agile while carrying his prey, which meant he could complete the cycle faster, taking it to the high branches.

The ideas flickered through Eagle's mind. His mind was a cold place, but that was good with him, a predator's mind needed to be sharp and cold, capable only of what he needed to do to survive.

Thoughts of humanity needed to be excised from his mind. He'd never been one for kindness anyway. Kindness was fake.

Circling up in the skies, seeking the weak, targeting them, removing them - that was real.

That was what nature told him to do. It was what he had to do.

Eagle felt purpose take hold of him, the ache to kill taking hold of him.

He needed to kill again.

He needed to be pure, to be hard. He needed to make himself one with the bird of prey. To be the mighty predator.

He needed to absorb his victim's life force, and to soar.

Tonight, he would do it again.

CHAPTER NINE

Katie approached the first of the foremen in the construction group that was working to fell and remove the trees on the site's northern border. She hoped that if the killer was hiding among this group, she would be able to pinpoint him. Already she had gained some insight into him, though not yet enough.

Katie knew that this was a cunning, careful man. They were seeking someone who thought differently, so differently that Katie had no idea what was motivating him, what was driving him to commit these weird murders.

Scenarios that placed him at risk as well. Treetops were complex, dangerous places to dump a body. What did it mean? What should she look for? She felt strongly that this killer was so different that he would come across as not quite normal. She didn't think he would appear ordinary or be able to hide within society without showing some signs of who he really was.

She would need to look out for those warnings. A big red flag would be a previous criminal record, and that would be an important starting point. The thoughts simmered in her mind as she approached the construction site.

She was on her own. Due to the sheer volume of the project, she and Leblanc were interviewing the different groups of subcontractors separately. However, they had decided that if either of them identified a suspect, they would go after him together.

"I don't want either of us at risk," Leblanc had said, and Katie knew from the look he had given her, that this was more than just professional concern.

Katie was his lover now. Leblanc had lost one lover in a dangerous situation. She understood his need to protect his partner.

And in the cases they handled, it was always a wise decision. The only thing she hoped he wouldn't do was to endanger himself looking to protect her.

She couldn't handle the thought of him being harmed, either.

The foreman of the crew walked over to her, an inquiring expression on his face. Katie nodded a greeting to the tall, rugged man.

"You're here asking questions about the murders?" he confirmed. "I couldn't believe it when I heard about Ms. Hughes. I didn't know her very well, but she had a good name in our industry. It's terrible to think about it and I can see my crew is distracted; they're discussing it nonstop. Do you know anything more about it?"

"It happened early this morning. The time of death was probably around five a.m., they think, as that's when she would have gone out walking. So we're looking for anyone who might have had an opportunity to be in the area and take her, at that time."

The foreman nodded. "Come into the break room. Let's talk there. It's quieter."

Katie thought that was a good idea. Out here, it was deafening.

He led the way to a large caravan. Katie looked dubiously at it, but inside, it was relatively soundproof and very cozy. The interior smelled deliciously of coffee. There were containers of donuts, muffins, sandwiches, and sodas. Easy, comforting calories for folk who worked long, late hours in adverse conditions.

There were a couple of people sitting around the small table. A couple more were squeezing through the narrow space on the way to another pocket-sized lounge.

"We've been working around the clock. I didn't handle last night's shift, but we had ten workers on site. I know them all from previous jobs. They would not have left our allocated site without signing out. We're extremely strict about that because of health and safety regulations, and because we don't want people shirking their job. Especially on night shift, that's always something we keep in mind."

"Understood," Katie said.

"So I can confirm that last night, the ten workers who did night shift worked throughout the night. They have their allocated breaks, which they are legally compelled to take. Two half-hour breaks in a twelve-hour shift. We staggered those. On the first break, they all sign out, leave the site, and get dinner from the main canteen. On the later break, they grab coffee and donuts in this caravan. We have a gas heater in there. There's a smoking zone just outside the site border, which is the only place our people can smoke. They're not allowed to build fires, or smoke elsewhere in the woods. That's a no-no as we don't want to be responsible for a major fire outbreak in the area. That caused a problem on a previous building site a couple of years ago, where half the forest went up, and so restrictions are much tougher now. Again, limited reasons to go off site. That's just how it works. In the small hours of the morning, everyone's tired. It's cold, the breaks are short. The guys just want to finish up and be done."

"So you are sure nobody left without permission or signing out?"

"Ma'am, I guarantee that. The boss on site last night has been working with me for ten years and he's just as strict as I am. Our crew doesn't spend time on site after work, they sleep off site. We do two transport shifts a day, taking them to and from a motel in a neighboring town."

"They couldn't sneak back here?" Katie asked.

He shook his head. "They don't have transport, and the town where we have accommodated them is too far from here to walk, that's for sure."

"Any of your crew have criminal records or been in trouble with the law?"

"No. Not this year. Last year, we did hire a couple of bad apples. We regretted the decision. We didn't rehire them. Our guys are clean. No previous problems."

Katie considered his words. It was sounding like this site was tightly managed.

"Did you see anyone lurking around? Anyone who your crew didn't recognize?"

"No. We haven't seen any strangers nearby. To be honest, most of the time, we're too busy to be looking into the woods, especially when it's dark. We're focused on our job. The lights shine inward, onto the work site, they don't shine outward into the trees. And I personally haven't seen anyone nearby, thanks to the warning notices on all the incoming roads and trails, telling people that access to the site is forbidden for safety reasons unless you're a registered worker."

"And strangers on site?"

"It would be very unusual to see a stranger on the site itself. Everyone on site wears their staff cards on display, and of course the correct safety equipment including reflective jackets at all times, and lights on the helmets at night. It gets so that you notice immediately if anyone doesn't have it, because everyone does. So on site, I can confirm everyone is legitimately accounted for."

Katie nodded. That made sense.

Unfortunately it wasn't what she wanted to hear. It was making it less likely that anyone on site was the killer. Everything was sewn up. Organized. Regulated. The site bosses were alert, and the signing out processes seemed to be rigorously adhered to. This was why the killing scene had been so shocking, because it was so unexpected. It was not something that she had instinctively expected to see after having witnessed the order of the construction site. Loud, noisy, but well run.

What did this mean? She didn't know. She felt at an absolute loss. But she knew they had better start thinking of alternative suspects, because the construction site itself might prove to be a dead end.

"Thank you," Katie said.

She turned and left. Her only hope was that Leblanc might have found a better lead. But the problem was that this was clearly a very well run operation. It was a tightly planned government project and the stakeholders involved were holding themselves accountable for its success. Everyone was keen to impress and do the best job, in the hope of earning more of those sought-after state dollars in the future.

It was going to be very hard to find a loophole or inconsistency in the way things were done.

Katie walked out, telling herself that she wasn't giving up.

She headed over to speak to Leblanc, who was walking out of the neighboring site. As she headed over to him, she noted that he looked discouraged.

"I've got nothing," he said to her, the moment he reached her.

"Why? What was the outcome?"

He shrugged. "There wasn't a lot of room for error. Things are efficiently run. The woman I spoke to told me she couldn't believe how organized the site is. She used to work elsewhere, and this is a lot better. She said their crew do sleep in camps on site, and could go into the woods at night if they wanted, but they have never had any problems or trouble in the past, and there are no workers with criminal records."

"I heard the same," Katie said. "The crew I visited sleep off site, but otherwise, similar circumstances."

"So, theoretically, it could have been an on-site worker who was off shift, but you would have to find the right individual, with a motive or a criminal record. There are hundreds of these workers. We can't question every one. It will take weeks, and it might well be that none of the site workers are guilty of it anyway.

As they walked, they were heading back toward the main buildings, feeling gloomily thoughtful, walking in step without even realizing it.

"I'm not sure where else we could try," Leblanc said.

"One thing we can do now, here, is ask the site to tighten up on protocols for the night. They need to take their security another notch up, especially for female workers. Perhaps they can be housed in town overnight. I'm sure they could provide additional lighting, and shine some lights into the woods as a deterrent. And when people move around off site, they must move around in pairs. Those parameters could at least save lives," Katie said. "We don't want this killer taking another victim. If we can prevent this, we must."

"I guess so." Leblanc sounded as demoralized as she felt. This was suddenly feeling like an impossible task, and even though Katie knew that investigations went this way and then veered back into better territory, it didn't help the feeling at the time.

And then, a woman's voice behind her said, "Excuse me."

Katie swung around, feeling surprised.

Behind her stood a tough looking woman in her thirties. Her face looked familiar, and thinking back, Katie realized she'd seen her in the caravan. She'd been sitting over coffee.

"The bosses sent out a message earlier, saying you were going to be on site, and that we should approach you or call you if we have any information," the woman explained.

"That's correct," Katie said. She felt encouraged that Carver had sent the word out so fast, and that it had brought results.

"I have something I think you need to know," the woman said, with a furtive glance back toward the site where she'd been working. "If I tell you, will it remain confidential?"

"I promise that anything you tell us will remain confidential," Katie said to the construction worker, feeling excitement simmering inside her. This woman had felt strongly enough to leave her workplace and chase after them after having gotten the message that they were seeking information. This was exactly what might progress the case further.

CHAPTER TEN

"Tell me who you are?" Katie invited, wanting to get the woman feeling more at ease, as she was now fidgeting nervously and seeming unsure of where she should start.

"I'm Petra Juarez. I've been working for these contractors for two years. I don't want you to think I am complaining, and I really don't want to get into trouble. I like my job. The guys are good people. We're all here because we want to make a good life for ourselves. A better life than we can make anywhere else."

"And are you familiar with the area?"

"This is my first project this far north. The others have been further south."

"And who is the person you suspect?"

Petra glanced around again, as if fearful someone was listening.

Katie glanced around too. Thanks to the background din, nobody was within earshot.

"It's not a member of our crew, but someone who's working alongside us for now," Petra said. "He is an arborist. And ever since we've been thrown together on this project, I've found him very disrespectful. Then, the other day, he did something out of line, I thought."

She glanced back again and this time, Katie detected fear in her gaze.

"What did he do to you?"

"The first time we met, it was like he definitely took notice of me. And then, a few days later, he started chatting me up. In this horrible, intimate, sort of creepy way. Asking me if I wanted to spend time with him, saying I was like a cute little chick, like a really hot little bird. Asking if I wanted to be caught in his net, trapped in his cage. Weird stuff like that. He was basically asking me to sleep with him. It was inappropriate. It was way out of line."

"What did you do?" Katie asked, feeling concerned, but also intrigued by the words this man had used. They seemed to her to relate to this case. Birds, nets, cages. The terminology was similar.

"I told him I wasn't interested. I didn't do it in an aggressive way. I had no desire to cause a fight. But this guy was extremely persistent. He kept on trying to touch me, to grab my hands. I mean, on a construction site, don't you think it's dangerous to behave that way?"

"For sure it is," Katie said.

"I have been trying to get through the day without being grabbed or touched. At the same time, I haven't wanted to cause a scene. I don't understand why he is still being so persistent after I'd made it clear I'm not interested."

"So, has he been pushing it further?"

"He tried again this morning. And I said no again. This time, I wasn't polite about it. And he reacted really badly. He lost his temper and said I would pay for this, that I was going to learn what would happen if I caused him to show his bad side. He said he would hurt me, that I'd regret it."

Katie felt deeply concerned by this. It was exactly the kind of scenario that could potentially explode. And this was exactly the kind of person she was looking for. Someone who could not control their impulses, who was showing themselves to be violent. A person who took what they wanted, by force if needed.

"Who is he?" she asked.

"His name is Michael Lone."

"Did you report his actions?"

She sighed. "I wanted to. I know I should have. But I was afraid of him. I was afraid of him doing something bad to me if I reported him," Petra admitted. "So I have said nothing. He knows I've said nothing. I think he knows I'm scared."

"Did you see him interacting with Clarissa Hughes at all?" Katie asked, wondering if this suspect had direct contact with the victim before her death.

"The surveyor who was killed? I didn't know her name. But yes, I saw him hounding her a couple of days ago when she was working in the same area as him. She was quite new on site and I am sure that made her attractive to him."

Katie raised her eyebrows at this information.

"Is Michael Lone working on site today?" Leblanc asked.

"Yes, he is. We work the same shifts. The same hours. He's working on the borders of the site at this time, taking a look at the trees, deciding if any further trees should be removed or if any are damaged."

"What does he look like?"

"He's a tall man, dark haired, with a ponytail. He wears yellow gloves while he works, and he should be down that way." She pointed.

"We will go and speak to him," Katie decided. "I'm very grateful that you decided to tell us this. It might be helpful to the case."

"I hope so. But please, leave my name out of it," she entreated. "If he does not get arrested, we still have to work together."

"We'll keep it totally confidential," Katie said. "I promise you that."

She took a deep breath. "I've said too much already. I don't want to get in trouble. I hope I haven't made a mistake."

Katie felt furious that anyone should have to be so scared for their safety that they begged the police to leave their name out of it, or worried about facing these consequences. But at the same time, she understood. She knew that the police didn't have the resources to ensure everyone's safety.

And she felt immensely grateful to Petra for coming forward with the information.

"I absolutely understand," she promised. "We will not mention your name, and we will make sure that you are not implicated in any way."

"Thank you," Petra said, relief showing on her kind, tan face.

Katie didn't want to delay any further. She knew they needed to go and speak to Michael Lone immediately. It was time to drill down into this arborist's reasons for his behavior. It wasn't so much his propositioning of Petra that was ringing alarm bells. It was his threats to her.

A threat to assault or kill someone was a clear indication of a potential psychopathic mind. It showed that the arborist was thinking in criminal terms

That was a sign that the man was violent, and if he was prepared to carry out his threats, then such an individual could quickly escalate to murder.

Katie and Leblanc spoke together as soon as Petra had walked away.

"I don't want to give away that she told us about him," Katie insisted firmly. "That's going to put her in danger and jeopardize her job if it turns out he is not the killer."

"So, how do we do it?" Leblanc asked.

Katie considered their options.

"This man is clearly disrespectful to women. If I approach him on my own, and try to question him, he might show me the same behavior."

Leblanc nodded in approval. "So basically, you go in and you aim to let his own behavior trap him."

"Exactly," she agreed. "I go in, cross-examine him, push his buttons, see if I can take him over the edge."

"So what do you want me to do?"

"I'd like you to stay further back and observe," she said. "If you're there, we probably won't get the same reaction out of him. But if he does try anything, then you can be ready to jump in and help manage the situation."

Leblanc nodded. "I can do that. I'll set up somewhere to observe."

"Then let's action our plan now," Katie said.

She spoke with more confidence than she felt.

Pushing this guy's buttons was going to take skill, judgment, and Katie knew she'd have to be on the alert for a physical attack as well.

But it would all be worth it if this violent and manipulative man proved to be the killer.

Katie walked back into the construction site, put on her most innocent expression, and headed over to the arborist's workplace.

CHAPTER ELEVEN

The first thing Katie noticed as she approached Michael Lone was that he fit the physical parameters they were looking for. He was at work on site, in his hard hat and reflective jacket, wearing yellow gloves. Tall, lean and sinewy, she could see his arms were strong as he stood, busy clipping away at the undergrowth surrounding a tree with a sharp pair of shears. He wore big, heavy boots.

The noise of the manual blades felt somehow vicious and repetitive, a sharp clear sound over the hum and crackle of the background noise.

Katie walked up to him with a friendly smile.

"Good afternoon. Mr. Lone?"

He turned and she saw his immediate scowl as he took her in. She instantly sensed contempt in his demeanor. This man was not respectful of women, that was clear.

"That's me. What is it?" he demanded.

She looked at him but he would not meet her gaze. His eyes were shifty and his own stare slid away from hers. In fact, to her surprise, he then turned back to the bushes he was working on, as if she wasn't there at all.

"Mr. Lone" she said again, louder.

"Yeah?" he asked.

"I'm from the FBI. We're investigating the murders."

"Murders?" He looked at her with impatience in his eyes. "We only had one worker murdered, and most likely that woman got herself in trouble of some kind. The other was some random hiker that got herself killed. Are you going to start interrupting our work for every death and killing that takes place in northern Minnesota?"

Katie narrowed her eyes. For sure, this man was a bully and he was using sarcasm as a weapon. But why was he fighting? What was he hiding?

"Did you know the victim?" she asked.

He shrugged. "I might have met her once or twice."

He wasn't admitting to hounding her. Katie pushed further.

"Did you speak to her in the past days? Why would you say she would be in trouble that would get her killed? Did she maybe reject you at all?"

He was silent, and Katie felt something shift in the atmosphere between them. He was suddenly on the defensive.

His expression shuttered, and she noticed him flexing his fingers. She didn't know if it was a sign of aggression or if he was just trying to get the feel of the shears right again.

"I'm just guessing what happened. I don't know for sure," he said abruptly. "I had nothing to do with it."

"Are you sure you didn't have any words with her before her death?" Katie was going to pressure him. She was going to drill down into this defensiveness.

"What are you implying, lady? Are you looking to try and blame me for what happened? Because if so, this conversation is over." He spoke in a low growl.

"This is not a conversation. You're being asked questions about a crime by an FBI agent, which you are obliged to answer," Katie reminded him. His attitude was completely disrespectful.

"If I don't like the person, I won't talk to them. I don't care if you're the FBI or not."

"I'm an FBI official, and you will answer my questions," Katie said coldly. "We have reason to believe that you might have something to do with these murders. This is not a request. It's an order. You can choose whether we have the conversation here, or whether I take you somewhere else."

"You have no reason to believe I harmed her," he snarled. Suddenly he dropped the shears with a clatter onto the ground.

"You are wasting my time," he snarled. "And I don't have to answer your questions." For sure, this situation was reaching a head, Katie thought. Her persistence was triggering him big-time, and just now, it was going to reach a point where he showed himself for what he was.

Katie was about to push the issue further, but then he snapped around to face her. "I didn't even know the woman. Why would I kill her? Now get out of my space." His voice rose to a shout.

Angrily, he stepped forward. He grabbed Katie by her shoulder, twisting his fingers hard into her upper arm as he shoved her away.

Caught off balance, Katie stumbled, slipping on the uneven, stony ground and going down on one hand before recovering herself. She jumped up into a crouch, ready to defend herself if he was going to attack.

But she didn't need to. Leblanc had been watching from nearby, and as the man took another swing at Katie, Leblanc burst out from the woods behind him.

As Leblanc charged at Lone, the arborist whirled around, looking shocked at his sudden arrival. Katie watched the bullying expression vanish from his face as if it had been wiped away. A moment later, Leblanc's fist slammed into his jaw.

Katie was surprised by how easily he lost his footing. Lone simply tipped over, and went sprawling back into the ragged, half-chopped shrubs.

"You do not assault an officer of the law," Leblanc roared.

Quickly, while the man was sprawled in the greenery, Katie grabbed his arms and got them behind his back. He was half dazed from the blow, but she was surprised by the wiry strength in his arms. He wriggled and struggled, trying to get free. He gave her a strangled sound, almost like a grunt of pain. Maybe it was a sound of frustration, she thought.

"Get off me!" the man snarled.

"You're interfering with a police operation," Leblanc snarled. "I'll do what I like."

"You can't do that. There's no law that says you can come out here and harass us." Lone sounded almost hysterical.

But Leblanc had clearly had enough of this behavior. He hauled him to his feet, and rammed him back hard against the thick trunk of the closest tree. Then he jerked him around, and this time, the fight had gone out of him enough for Katie to get the handcuffs on him.

She noticed he was favoring one leg, standing with all his weight on his left leg. Perhaps Leblanc had injured him worse than she'd thought.

She was breathing hard. This was a violent man. He hadn't hesitated to rush in and assault her. Quickly, and without any compunction, he'd chosen to attack, and she wondered what that meant for the case.

"This is a set up, you bastards," he snarled at them. "You're framing me. I'm not going to stand for this. You could have broken my jaw. In fact you might have done so."

"You chose to attack Agent Winter," Leblanc spat at him. Katie could see there was a lot of anger in him. She'd seen the force he'd put behind that blow. It was more than necessary. Leblanc had let out some

51

of the anger he was carrying inside him, the pain and guilt from being unable to defend his previous partner. That troubled her, but on the other hand, she reasoned with herself, it had been a violent attack and he was entitled to retaliate with force.

It was time to question this man thoroughly now. The only problem was that they were too far from any police department to take him in. In this isolated site, they were going to have to make another plan.

"We could go in there, I guess," Katie suggested, glancing at the nearby container halfway up the hillside, which looked to be used as a temporary office.

"Come along with us," Leblanc snarled at Lone.

Katie grabbed his cuffed hands and hustled him along. He was definitely limping, she saw. When they reached the container office, she walked ahead of the men, quickly pushing inside.

Two women working in there, hunched over a plastic desk, looked up in surprise.

"What's going on?" the closer woman questioned, sounding worried.

"We need to use this space for a few minutes, if you don't mind," Katie said. "It's to ask some questions in connection with the murders we're investigating."

"Sure, sure." Quickly, the women stood up, scrabbling their belongings together and cramming them into bags. With a curious glance at the suspect waiting outside, they left the office.

"Can't you stop them?" Lone screeched. "They can't do this to me! I didn't do anything!"

Without answering him, they grabbed their coats and hurried away into the windy evening, looking alarmed and unsettled at what was playing out.

Katie was wondering how much of a reputation Lone had earned among the workers, that the foreman and manager might not know about. Brute force and intimidation could be effective weapons in silencing people.

Leblanc hustled Lone inside, pushing him down on the plastic chair that the closest woman had just vacated.

The office smelled of coffee, and a faint, rich tinge of heated-up food. Very different from the usual sterile environment of the interview rooms Katie used.

They knew already that their suspect was violent, and that he had issues with women, and that he had no inhibitions about physically attacking another person. At this construction site, Katie hoped, they would be able to find out how far these violent tendencies had taken him, and whether he was a killer.

CHAPTER TWELVE

Now that he was being formally questioned, in a two against one situation, Katie saw that the aggression had gone out of the arborist. Lone no longer looked defiant and aggressive. Instead, he looked surly and defensive.

He was a typical bully, Katie realized, a man who would capitalize on the vulnerability of others just because he could.

She detested his type. But Katie knew that she had to remain cool minded and objective. She could not allow her own personal dislike for this bullying, misogynistic man to influence her approach to the case.

He was either guilty or he was not. She would have to go forward with an unemotional approach.

But although she was not going to mention Petra's name, she still felt suspicious about those terms of endearment that this man had used when trying to bully her into sleeping with him. He'd referred to being caught in his net, trapped in his cage, which made her wonder if that manner of hiding the bodies had been on his mind.

But she was determined to find it out in a calm way.

Leblanc had clearly not yet returned to that level of mental equilibrium. He was still fuming, and letting Lone know it.

"Why did you assault Agent Winter?" Leblanc demanded, keeping his voice low and threatening.

"I didn't," Lone whined at him. "I never did. You're framing me. I'm not going to take this."

Lone struggled to get up out of the chair, but Leblanc was too fast for him. He leaned across, and forced the suspect back down into his seat.

"You're going to sit quietly and answer the questions," Leblanc assured him.

"If you are reasonable, and answer truthfully, this will go much more smoothly," Katie advised him. "If you are evasive and you keep on trying to fight us, you might be here all night. Who knows? We might even need to keep you from your shift tomorrow. In that case, your bosses will be informed."

If he was guilty of murder, that would be an insignificant factor. But if he wasn't, then he wouldn't want to get into trouble that he couldn't handle in his own aggressive, forceful way. Being in trouble with bosses, and missing a shift because of his own bad behavior, would affect his pocket.

Katie watched him think about the situation. At least he was, finally, thinking.

"What do you want to know?" he snapped out after a pause.

"Let's start with your movements over the past two days. When were you on site? When were you off site? Did you travel with any other crew?"

"I'm not part of that contractor's team. I sleep here, on site," Lone said defensively.

That was significant. Being on site after his working hours, as a lone operator who was not part of a crew, meant he would have had the chance to take a victim last night.

"Where do you sleep?" Katie asked.

"There's a tented camp set up. About thirty of us are there, on the western side of the site."

"Including Clarissa Hughes?" Katie asked.

He shook his head. "Women and married couples are in the temporary cabins. Those are on the south side, they're more sheltered and they have better ablution facilities."

"What security keeps you in your camp at night?"

Lone sighed. "None, agent. There are site rules which we abide by, but there is no security keeping us here. Why should there be? It's not a prison camp. And it's miles from anywhere."

"Is there any night security on the site?" Katie asked.

"No. There's no night security. It's a construction site in the middle of nowhere! What are you trying to do? Get me fired?" He leaned forward and glared at her, as if he could intimidate her into backing down.

"Not at all. I am just trying to find out if you had an opportunity to visit the temporary cabins."

"No. I didn't go there. And if you want proof of that, you can ask the guys I share with. I was in there all night. I share the tent with another guy."

Katie wasn't going to take a shared tent as an alibi. Especially given the fact the tents would undoubtedly have private compartments separated from each other, and that construction workers after a long day slept soundly at night, and also that Lone was a bully who could easily coerce someone into agreeing with his version.

"A shared tent is not sufficient proof of innocence."

Now Lone was starting to look panicked.

"What is? I mean, what the hell do you guys even need? What must I do, or are you just going to arrest me? Am I allowed to get anyone else in on this? A lawyer, or what?"

He was clearly used to people caving in to whatever he said or did.

"What about tree climbing. Do you do that?"

He shook his head. "I can't climb any longer. I'm ground staff only."

"Why's that?" Katie asked. Finally there was a fact that might just shed more light on his guilt, or innocence.

"Because two years ago, I had a very bad fall from a tree. I destroyed my right ankle. It was touch and go whether they amputated below the knee. I had shattered bones, torn tendons and ligaments. They plated it back together but I have to wear an ankle brace all day at work, as well as reinforced safety boots." He bent down and slapped the thick sides of the boots he wore. "Even with the boots, my ankle can't hold anything except a direct weight, flat on the floor. Any sideways pull, and there's a risk the tendons would rupture again."

"Do you have proof of this?" Leblanc queried.

"Sure. I can show you all the medical reports, the certificates reassigning me. If I fall again, from any height, I lose my foot. The ankle's weak and if it breaks again, it's tickets. You might have noticed that I fell over when you hit me. That's because it can't support me. If someone hits me, I fall. I'm used to it. So thanks, but no thanks. If this killer climbed a tree, it wasn't me. Not only would I not kill another person, despite what you think of me, but I most definitely would not risk the job I have, and the use of my leg, doing some crazy climb at night."

"Show me the information," Katie asked, with a glance at Leblanc. She could see he thought the same. A catastrophic injury of that nature would rule this man out. And she had found his responses during the fight to be strange, the way he'd collapsed when he'd been hit.

Undoubtedly, the killer would have needed great strength and flexibility in both ankles in order to wedge his feet into the crevices of the branches, and ascend a tree in the dark, while carrying the full weight of a body. It was not something that a person with a compromised ankle could do. Or would do, given the high risk of re-injury.

"You can talk to the medical people if you want. I don't know what more I can do to prove my innocence. I had nothing to do with those girls disappearing. Like I said, they probably just made the wrong guy angry at them." His trademark scorn was back again as his confidence returned.

He handed over his phone, and Katie accessed the folder. She raised her eyebrows.

This had been a catastrophic injury. It most definitely had impacted his physical scope.

Personally, if she had been injured in such a way, Katie thought she would also have made a point of not getting into fights where the ankle could be hurt worse. But perhaps that was just her personal view, she thought wryly.

At any rate, he was cleared.

"You can go," she said.

He got up and walked out without another word, stepping carefully on his right ankle. Katie scowled at him. He was a deeply unpleasant person and she made a note to mention this to Carver, giving him an update on the behavior and conduct of this man. She hoped the site boss would be able to discipline him, or at any rate keep a closer eye on him while he was here.

She made a face at Leblanc. "It would have been nice to get this solved today," she said.

"I know," he agreed. "It's getting into night now, and I'm worried that by the morning, given this guy's short interval, we might have another victim."

Katie shook her head. "I am absolutely not going to allow that to happen. We need to get some protocols in place to keep people safe."

"Good idea," Leblanc said.

"I want to speak to Carver anyway, now, to tell him about Lone. But we can also discuss site safety for tonight. I think that from now, this site must be on full lockdown until morning. Every female worker must go in pairs when they go anywhere. We need extra lighting at all the exit points leading to the woods. And we need as much security as possible, even if it's volunteers working on a rotational basis."

As she spoke, Leblanc was typing the points into his laptop.

"Let's go and speak to him about this," he said. "He's a good manager. Chances are he's already thought of some of this, but perhaps there are some additional safety points here he can use."

"I am not going to let another person lose their life tonight. Not if I can help it," Katie emphasized.

But in the pit of her stomach, she felt a chill that couldn't be banished.

This killer was clever, cunning and careful. And they knew so little about him.

She felt afraid that despite their most stringent precautions, he might find a way to strike again before the morning.

CHAPTER THIRTEEN

Eagle knew they were trying to stop him. Of course they were. Birds of prey were often not loved. They could be trapped, hunted, chased away by people in their anger and fear.

But it didn't stop the kill. Of course not. A bird of prey was strong and powerful, persistent and cruel. And he would be, too. He had to be. To become what he desired, he had to prove he was as tenacious, as vicious, as the deadliest predator.

He perched in a treetop, the night air cool on his skin, observing the site from the darkness of the woods as he decided on his approach.

The campsite was a porous structure. It could not be fully fenced. It was too enormous. They'd done their best with the camps, he saw. Glaring lights were now directed into the forest, and there was little movement in the closest camp.

Needing a better view, he climbed down from the tree and began pacing silently around the perimeter, staying back, avoiding those piercing lights. They'd put up temporary gates. He didn't see any of the women walking alone. In fact, an hour ago, a bus had arrived at the gate. He'd seen the women board the bus, carrying bags. Those women who had been sleeping on site were going into town. They were being hidden away, kept in their cages for tonight for their own protection. Being kept safe from him.

The thought didn't bother him, rather the opposite. It gave him a surge of power. He was the one creating this fear. Not even the sight of the circling predator, but simply the knowledge of it, was causing people to hide.

And not only on the site, it seemed. The forest itself felt quiet. Outside of the chaos of construction, he'd picked up no movement. No runners nearby, no people hiking innocently through. Those times, for now, were over. He sensed that.

The neighboring towns were aware, he was certain. The first woman he'd picked off, running through - that had been lucky, and he would not be so lucky again.

They thought they knew him. They did not know him at all.

59

He was only now beginning to know himself. To understand who he was and what he could do, and more than that. Who he needed to become.

He needed to approach more carefully, to plan in advance.

Just as the moon had disappeared behind clouds, he would disappear. He would wait, and watch, and then, when he was ready, he would strike. Because for every ten fearful people, one would be careless. That was human nature.

He had never felt so alive as he did now. All his senses were on high alert. He stepped soundlessly through the woods, invisible, unseen. Nobody knew he was here. Nobody even sensed him.

He was the ghost. The predator's shadow. He was the one who was hunting.

He would only strike when he was absolutely sure. But one thing was certain. He would strike again. Tonight. He couldn't afford to miss a night.

Abruptly, he sensed another presence nearby.

He froze, startled. It wasn't another human. It was large, but it was not a human.

It was a bear. Instantly, Eagle drew back, blending into the darkness.

It was a large bear, forging through the forest some distance away. A grizzly. It was a powerful presence, and it would do him no good to fight or chase it away. Bears were territorial, especially in spring. It might be attracted by the leftover food, by the rubbish and leavings that this development brought with it. Hungry in the spring, it would be looking to scavenge. This bear would defend its territory, and it would not be afraid of him.

Slowly, the bear walked by. It turned briefly and seemed to look at him. He sensed the animal's interest in him. He had a powerful presence, too.

Quickly, nimbly, he swung into the nearest tree. He could climb anything. Climbing on his own was easier than climbing with prey. In a moment he was ten feet up, then fifteen, clambering silently to the slimmer branches where the bear could not follow. The canopy barely shook.

Eagle stayed there, perfectly still, perfectly aware.

He watched the beast go by. He saw the bear's massive shoulders and head disappear into the darkness.

With the bear safely gone, Eagle's thoughts returned to his prey.

They would have anticipated him, taken precautions. They would have spent time and effort, searching for clues to find him, seeking his presence.

But he had one advantage. He knew the layout of the site. He knew who would be working where.

There was one particular area, to the north of the site, where they were working overnight. They were on a very tight schedule and they had fallen behind. They were working at speed. Bonuses were being offered for working overtime, he'd heard talk of that. Word got around, and he had sharp, keen ears that could pick up these whispers.

Human or animal, Eagle had an advantage. He was a predator. He knew what he was, what he had to hunt, to kill, to survive.

This was his hunting ground. He crept closer, listening to the shouts and cries, the scream of the chainsaws.

He knew exactly what he was waiting for.

A man headed out of the site, dusting his hands, whistling. He was in the woods to smoke. This was the designated smoking area that they had demarcated for this part of the site, which backed onto a clearing surrounded by smaller trees.

The acrid fragrance of the cigarette wafted over and Eagle breathed it in.

This man was not a suitable target for him. He was too big, too bulky. He was a hefty, strong, burly man. Eagle had seen him many times in the past few days, and knew he was one of the most skilled chainsaw operators.

But that was the thing about smokers. They congregated.

In a minute, there was a tread of footsteps, and Eagle saw his prey arrive. His heart quickened.

This was the perfect target for him. A slim, smaller man, with narrow shoulders. A little mouse of a man. He was one of the machine operators, who could shunt the powerful machinery to and fro at top speed, scooping up and loading the logs.

He heard the flick of a lighter. And their low voices.

"Terrible thing these murders. Even my wife's gone back into town," the big man said. "They won't let any spouses stay overnight."

"Yeah," the slim man said sourly. "And now we're all suffering, losing our privileges, getting locked down. No more of this, no more of that. Women shouldn't be on a site like this anyway."

"They've got every right," the big man said defensively. "My wife handles all the catering for our group."

"I'm saying, I don't think they belong here. It's a man's world out here. Look what they've brought us. Nothing but trouble."

Listening, Eagle smiled, almost suppressing a laugh because the man was so wrong. And best of all, he was annoying his co-worker.

"If you say so, then that's your call," the big man said angrily. Eagle heard the stomp of his boot on the cigarette butt and then he marched away.

The other man gave a breathy laugh, as if he'd gotten pleasure out of riling his colleague. Then he drew deeply on his cigarette again.

But Eagle was creeping closer.

He heard the man exhale, smelled the tang of smoke.

And then, he struck.

Fast. Powerful. Silent.

He had the man by the throat so quickly, so cruelly, that there was no time for him to struggle. His prey was totally subdued. His iron grasp - his talons - were unrelenting.

Within moments, the man stopped moving. He lay limp and lifeless in Eagle's grasp. It was the best kill yet, and exultation filled him at how he had learned and grown in this journey.

Nimbly, Eagle bent and hoisted the man onto his shoulder.

It was difficult to move fast and quietly carrying another's weight, and this prey was heavier than the previous two, but he managed it well. After all, he now had some experience. He was becoming more skilled. Adrenaline and elation gave him an additional burst of strength, and his victim felt light in his arms.

Now for the final arrangement, the placement of the body.

He wasn't going far. Just fifty yards away, he had the perfect tree in mind.

Eagle wondered how long it would take them to find this corpse and whether, by then, he'd have the chance to take another.

CHAPTER FOURTEEN

Exhausted from the day's efforts, and feeling demoralized by her lack of success, Katie waited at the motel desk to receive her room key.

This was the only motel in town. There were no others. And there was only one room available, because all the others were occupied by the female workers. A small group of them had just checked in, which Katie felt glad about.

People were taking the threat seriously.

The motel was buzzing. A few women were chatting in the lobby and the courtyard, speaking in concerned voices, pleased about the treat of this more luxurious night in town, but anxious about the killer.

She could hear the anxiety, tight and tense in their voices, as she and Leblanc walked to their room.

Katie couldn't wait to fall asleep in the comfort of Leblanc's arms, to feel his embrace, calming her after the frustrating day they'd had, and being able, in the moment, to forget her anxiety about what the future might hold.

"Should we grab some food?" Leblanc asked. "There's a diner across the road."

The diner, Katie amended, feeling a sudden flash of humor, a welcome lightness after the heaviness of the afternoon. It was the only one in town, and looked to be a pretty place. Someone had taken care over the outside decor, with whitewashed walls and flowers in planters.

"Let's do that," she agreed.

They went inside, sat down at a booth.

The place was packed, not only with women, but also with a handful of men who had come to town to see their wives and girlfriends.

Together, they sat, watching the passing traffic on the road outside, and listening to the buzz of conversation around them.

The blonde waitress bustled over, and they ordered the day's special - soup, toasted Reubens, and a piece of pie. Katie hadn't eaten all day. That calorie-packed menu sounded like exactly what she needed.

They ordered a bottle of water and two coffees.

"Coming right up," the waitress said with a smile. She looked excited that the place was so busy. Probably, Katie thought with a flash of sympathy, she felt she was playing an important role in the proceedings, making sure that everyone taking refuge in this busy diner got their food on time.

Katie couldn't share in her excitement. Until this killer was caught, she felt that every single person in this town might be at risk. Who knew where he would focus and who he would target next? What if he came into town to seek a victim?

She felt worried for this innocent waitress. Worried for every person in the diner, and everyone still on site.

"I wish we knew more about him," Katie said. She felt obsessed by this man, by who he was, by what motivated him.

"Perhaps, by tomorrow, we will," Leblanc agreed.

"I don't want him to take another victim. Leblanc, I want to get ahead of this guy."

"I want for Scott to be able to present this case as a success," he agreed.

Katie was one-hundred percent on board with that. She knew only too well what failure would mean. This was not the time to fail. Not when the fate of the task force hung in the balance.

"If we don't solve this fast, it's going to count against us. It's going to be used by the people who are making their power moves and playing their political games. I am absolutely certain about it," she said.

She felt dark thoughts clouding her mind. So many people were counting on them. Scott would be working late, she was sure of it, gathering all the information he could get his hands on, feeling as anxious as she was about the urgency of what they were dealing with.

She couldn't afford for this to fail. She had to get ahead of the game.

Katie knew it was going to be difficult. She felt as if she was waging a war on two fronts. Not only was she fighting the killer and his weird, twisted scenarios that were destroying lives, but also the threat to the task force coming from higher up. That would destroy her current workplace. It would destroy her relationship with Leblanc, and fling her out, to start again. It would mean abandoning the small comfort zone she'd finally begun to create for herself, after years of self-imposed loneliness and refusing to make anywhere a home.

"I agree with you," Leblanc said stonily. "Of course they will use it against us."

Katie knew that he saw things exactly the same way. It was obvious from his creased brow. He'd come to the same unavoidable conclusion.

If they didn't wrap this up fast, they both ran the risk of being made scapegoats.

The food arrived, the plates generous and surprisingly tasty. Katie dug in. Even though she felt an anxious twist in her stomach that curbed her appetite, she knew that she needed these calories. For what might follow, tonight or tomorrow, she needed to be fueled, strong and ready.

Tomorrow, she resolved, she was going to try and solve this. Whatever it took, and no matter what it took from her.

There was nothing to lose that wasn't already going to be lost if they didn't succeed.

*

Much later that night, she woke, curled in the comfortable motel bed. She gasped in a breath, reaching out to feel the warmth of Leblanc's arms as he held her instinctively, wanting to keep the nightmares at bay.

She was always haunted by them on a case.

Her eyes wide, she stared at the window, realizing that the first glow of morning light was starting to lighten the curtains.

She'd had one of the most vivid and disturbing dreams ever. In it, she'd been back in the cell, interviewing Everton, the serial killer who'd given her the lead to Gabriel Rath.

But Everton had been laughing at her this time.

"Oh, Katie," he jeered. "Did you think I was telling the truth? I didn't see Gabriel take Josie. Oh, no. Not at all. I saw him kill her! I watched him, as he murdered her, and then carried her body away to hide her."

"No," Katie had whispered in response. "No, it can't be! You're lying!"

But Everton had laughed, a cold, callous sound.

"If you can't handle the truth, don't ask for it," he whispered. And then he'd reached through the bars toward her. His hands had felt icy, as they had closed around her neck.

Shivering as she remembered that dream, Katie felt Leblanc squeeze her hand as he stirred drowsily beside her.

"It is getting light outside," he whispered.

The night had passed. What had it brought? A possibility of hope? Or another kill, and the stark realization that there was no way out of this?

At that moment, the trill of her phone broke the silence.

Feeling her heart start to pound, she reached for it and grabbed up the call as Leblanc snapped on the bedside lamp.

It was Scott.

"Morning, Scott." Her voice sounded hoarse with tiredness and strained with expectancy. Beside her, she felt Leblanc keep very quiet and still. Scott must not know they'd spent the night in the same room. Their relationship must remain a secret, even from their boss.

"Morning, Katie." Scott's voice was heavy. "Bad news. They've found another body. There's been another kill. Same M.O. but this time, a man."

"A man?" she gasped in surprise, seeing Leblanc's eyes widen in shock. Katie felt a chill like icy fingers running down her back. She felt like she was, once again, stumbling through the dark, and that she didn't know anything about this killer at all.

"You need to get to site, as soon as you can. We are racing against time here, and I mean this in more than one way."

Scott's voice was loaded with meaning and Katie felt all her fears about the future descend again.

He had struck again. He was ahead of them. And Katie sensed without a doubt that failure, on this case, meant that her whole world was going to change.

"We'll be there in twenty minutes," she said, pulling back the covers.

CHAPTER FIFTEEN

There was a different feel on site today. Katie picked it up immediately. Things were quieter. The frantic activity of yesterday was subdued. There were less noises emanating from the pockets of activity within the construction zone.

It was a feeling of fear. Word had spread. Everyone on site knew that a killer was now targeting people indiscriminately. Katie saw the bulk of this operation had actually shut down.

The attendant at the site gate waved them through hurriedly, as if hoping their presence here meant that things would soon be back to normal.

Katie wasn't so sure.

The local police were already on the scene. Sheldon was striding out of the woods, holding a roll of crime scene tape, looking frazzled and short on sleep. He strode over to them.

"I can't believe this. After all the security they added, all the precautions they took. It didn't help."

Katie shook her head. "Let's go see what played out this time, and how he managed to do it," she said quietly.

"It's this way," Sheldon said.

He walked across the site, heading west, to an area that Katie remembered as having been buzzing with frantic activity the day before.

Now, the site was quiet. All personnel had been ordered off it, clearly. Only Carver, the site manager, wearing a worried expression and also looking red-eyed, was standing there to meet them.

"The victim is Liam McInroy. He's been working for us for three years, age twenty-nine. He's one of our best machinery operators."

"What happened?" Katie asked.

"He went for a smoke. One of the chainsaw operators, Mark Edwards, had a few words with him. They were standing here, in the smoking zone. Edwards pointed the exact place out to me."

The manager paced a few steps away from the site. Katie followed.

She could see the tread of boots on the ground. So these men had walked off site for a smoke, believing that they would be safe.

"Edwards said that Liam was in a bad mood. He was angry that the site protocol had changed. He was being critical of women and blaming them for causing this. That annoyed Edwards and he cut his break short and went back to site, leaving Liam here alone."

"Go on?" Katie said.

"That must have been at about four a.m., but the problem is that the machinery had just been shut down for a couple of hours. So nobody noticed his absence until five-thirty a.m. when they started up again. They then figured out he'd last been seen going for a smoke." He pressed his lips together. "The guys couldn't think where he could be, but they did worry the worst had happened. They called me immediately. I ordered the teams to stop work, and we formed small groups and walked into the woods with flashlights, checking the treetops, just in case."

"And you found him?"

"Yes. We found him half an hour later." He shook his head hard.

"Is the body still there?" Katie asked.

"He's there. He's up in the tree. It's surreal. Bizarre. The pathologists are going to have to get a whole team in with ladders to remove him. A whole team. Because it's so high up and so dangerous. I can't believe this. The whole thing is just crazy. We're shutting down operations today. None of the guys are in the right mind frame to work now. Nobody's mind is on the job."

Katie could already see the bright flutter of crime scene tape, deep in the woods. Not wanting to ask Carver to come along with them and view the distressing scene again, she paced there on her own, with Leblanc behind her.

She stared up at the tree and her heart skipped a beat.

The sight of that body, curled up in the high fork of a tree, was deeply, viscerally distressing to her. It was just so wrong.

Hearing about it was different than looking at it. How had anyone even gotten up that tree?

She heard Leblanc hiss in an astonished breath as his thought processes followed the same path. It was as if this person was trying to shift reality.

That was Katie's most insistent thought and she clung to it, knowing that any impression she had now might be important and might lead somewhere. She desperately needed to get into this killer's mindset, and so far, she had no clue.

He was trying to shift reality. And he was going to serious efforts to do so. What she saw here was the work of someone who was thinking and striving for a scenario far removed from normalcy.

She could not see any signs of blood, and felt sure that this victim had been strangled, just the same as the others had.

"Have you spoken to Edwards, the man who was with him just before he died?" Katie asked Sheldon. As the last witness, and someone who had exchanged angry words, Edwards was potentially a suspect.

"Yes. I've spoken to him already. He was waiting for me when I arrived. He said he was only on his break for ten minutes. His coworkers were having coffee and were surprised he was back so soon. They confirmed the time he'd been away. It definitely rules out having taken a body up a tree."

"Yes, it does," Katie agreed.

So the person who had last seen Liam had not been responsible for his death.

But thinking about the scenario, Katie felt sure that the killer had planned this. Maybe not fine-tuned it, but he had been lurking, prowling around this particular site and waiting for someone of the right size and weight to take a smoke break alone.

He was intelligent, sly, observant.

And patient.

She stared up at the tree. The body was about thirty feet up. How had he managed to do that? Physically, it was a hard, dangerous challenge. Something difficult and demanding that he had to do, that he was striving for, that caused him suffering also. It was as if he was claiming a prize.

He was claiming this victim.

Katie's mind was racing. She gazed at the tree, feeling the presence of the killer, seeing him in her mind's eye.

She had no idea what his motivation was, but she sensed he was not just some crazy person out to cause harm. There must be a strange logic to his actions. It was as if he believed he had a right to do this, that he would be justified in taking these lives. He was doing this to make a point. He had a point to make.

She shivered. This person was solidifying in her head as someone who was serious, determined, and with a powerful sense of purpose.

He had struck again. He had won again.

And the killer was escalating. There was no doubt about it.

She could define all the parameters but she could not see where they led. That was beyond her powers right now.

She wondered if it would be possible to close the site completely. For everyone's safety, that would be best. But she guessed that logistically it might not be possible, with the scope and timeline of the operation and things having to happen in sequence, and the amount of machinery on site already. Never mind the political waves it would create, something that would not be wise for them now. All she could do was push forward as fast as possible and find this killer before he took any more victims.

"We are looking for someone damaged. Someone who is not normal. I am wondering if they appear normal or if they look different, too. Someone who is staying in the shadows and making themselves known, not for who they are but for what they can do."

"But who they are is the important thing," Leblanc added.

"He's in the area. He must know the area. He's an extremely talented climber. And he has a purpose, something that is forcing him to separate himself from humanity and to turn against it."

Katie narrowed her eyes.

It might not be much, but this was all she had.

But the fact he'd been lurking outside the site, presumably for some time, was a lead. That was something that could take them further.

She turned to Leblanc. An idea had occurred to her.

"We need to search wider than the site. Let's take a drive between here and town, and see if there's any other activity happening. Perhaps there's a team at work building a road, or laying a water pipe. Someone has had access to these woods for a few nights now, and has learned this construction site well. If it's not someone within the site itself, it might be someone who's working on a related project."

"I like that idea," Leblanc said.

Katie felt that widening the search was the next logical step, looking for other sites nearby where someone had the opportunity, the time, or the motive to lurk around the woods, waiting to pick off victims.

CHAPTER SIXTEEN

The aroma of well-brewed coffee hovered in the air of a boardroom that few people would ever step inside.

It was the private boardroom of the state governor, a man of immense personal wealth, and overarching political ambition.

Timms looked at the man himself, closely, as he ushered him inside. He took in his finely groomed silver hair, his white-toothed smile, his perfect, pale beige tan.

As one of the previous senior special agents in the FBI, Timms was practiced in the fine art of playing within the political arena.

It could be as deadly and dangerous a place as any combat site, given the circumstances. And today, Timms was unsure about the circumstances. It was as if they had all just been cast in a political drama that they could not control.

He walked inside, ahead of the governor, his feet treading over the plush carpet, and, just for a brief moment, wished that he was going to have this crucial conversation with someone whom he fully trusted.

But he did not trust the governor, although they were good friends. He'd always found him something of a loose cannon, and someone who rushed into decisions that should be carefully made and measured. He put ego over the greater good. And he was hugely, politically ambitious.

Timms thought that in the right circumstances, or the wrong ones, the man could be dangerous.

"Good to see you, Timms. Take a seat," the governor invited.

Timms lowered himself onto the plush leather sofa. An assistant poured coffee and passed him a plate of pastries.

"Good to see you, too. Thank you for making the time," Timms said respectfully.

At the same time, he had to admit, the governor's heart and sentiment were generally in the right place. He was not corrupt. Though egotistical and highly ambitious, he was also set on making the changes for the good that he believed needed to take place, and for most of these, Timms was in agreement. The changes would be for the greater good.

But along the way, like pawns in a game, some things were being sacrificed, and one of these was the cross border task force. The governor had a misconception about it and he was refusing to change his mind.

Timms was here to fight for Katie Winter and to push for the survival of a unit that he believed, implicitly, to be a great force for good.

A fifty-eight-year-old man with a tall physique and a strong jaw, the governor was an imposing figure. He was an astute politician and a man of powerful conviction. He had the air of a man who never needed to ask for help.

That was because, in most cases in his career, others were asking for his help.

But Timms had one bargaining chip that the others did not. He was personal friends with the governor.

He knew that could be a bad thing, and was not necessarily an advantage. Because friendship was a delicate balance. If destroyed, the implications could be far reaching.

More than the task force was at stake here and he knew he needed to proceed with caution.

Timms waited. He always let people make the first move in a conversation. He was a man who listened and observed.

That was how he'd gotten this far. There were few people who were better at seeing the road ahead and at making decisions on the spot.

"You don't have long with me. I have meetings in about thirty minutes," the governor warned.

"I know, I know," Timms assured him. "But I do have something very important to discuss with you."

The governor said nothing, just raised his eyebrows.

Timms took a deep breath. "I understand that you're looking to shut down the cross border task force."

"That's right. I am."

Timms decided it was time to play the good guy, the harmless guy, that likable person just pleading for balance.

"They're doing a great job. I've been following them closely."

"As have I," the governor countered.

His first line of attack was to establish the facts.

"You know the task force works across state boundaries," he said, making it clear that he knew what the governor already knew.

"I do."

"It has worked closely with the FBI. The actual cases they have worked on were the result of the two sets of skills and resources coming together. I believe, from my own experience, that the task force has been a success. The crimes have been solved, and the criminals apprehended."

The governor nodded. "I'm just not convinced that's the right solution. I am aware of the statistics in this area. I am also aware of the fact that the task force is a political hot potato. You know that as well as I do."

Timms drank his coffee. The governor was playing his cards close to his chest.

He knew the governor would never disclose his real reasons for wanting the task force gone. Not even to Timms. Probably, not even to his closest advisors. Not to the attendant in the corner of the boardroom who was recording the meeting and taking notes.

So the next few minutes were going to be spent in playing a risky game.

Timms had played this game with him before. He knew that the governor was not going to budge an inch on this one. He needed to get him to capitulate in other ways. He needed to get him to reverse his decision, or give him an opportunity for it to be saved, even if it took some manipulation.

Timms hoped he would be skilful enough to manage it.

"I'm aware that it has multiple political allegiances," he acknowledged, "but the reality is that it is working. It is solving crimes, and the public is being protected. It is a system that works. It is not just some gimmick. It's real. It's happened. And there is no way that we can put that back in the box."

"There's nothing the task force is doing, that the police can't do just as well. I've looked at the average timeframes. They are similar. It's overlapping, guzzling resources."

Timms knew the crimes the task force handled were far more complex and dangerous than many of the routine crimes the police dealt with. But by using the clever comparison of averages, the governor was discounting this advantage. Yet again, Timms realized how skilful and wily this man was.

"Governor, I'm not here to debate this with you. I'm here to plead my case. I am asking that you reconsider your position on the task force."

"That's not going to happen. The task force is going to be disbanded. I'm really sorry, Timms. I know that you probably have personal friends within it, but they're good agents, right? They'll be deployed elsewhere?" Now the governor was frowning at him, and Timms saw he'd had enough. He had only moments left before this meeting was declared over.

It was time to play the final card. The only card he had left.

"Are you aware what they are doing now? The crime they're investigating?"

"No. I'm not aware."

"Right now, they are busy working on a series of murders that are taking place in Minnesota, close to the border."

The governor of Minnesota was one of this man's close allies and good friends. He'd been one of the first to do a turnaround, agree with him, and oppose the task force.

"They're a weird and disturbing series of murders, and they are the type of crimes that can capture the public's attention in an instant. They can cause a massive amount of negative press. At the moment, we're keeping a lid on it."

"On what?"

"On the fact that the murders are taking place at the new construction site in northern Minnesota. I know that's one of the most important projects that the government in that state has on the go. It's going to make a massive difference in the state. In fact, you could even call it a flagship project, setting the standards for others. Now, it's getting delayed. It's hemorrhaging money. Nobody has a clue what's going on. Fear is spreading."

The governor was frowning now, looking anxious for the first time so far.

"The task force are there. They are trying to hunt down one of the most dangerous, most elusive serial killers that I know of. They're working around the clock, putting themselves at serious risk, taking things beyond the places where the police have expertise. Even the most senior police."

"I've seen the reports come in. I haven't read them yet." He glanced at a folder on the table.

Timms could see the man was now concerned

"The task force are saving the state money by getting this solved. They are saving the police time. And, of course, saving lives," he pleaded.

74

The governor took out the folder, opened it, scanned through the reports. His frown deepened.

"They are going to solve this," Timms emphasized. "They will get this operation back on track. You know and I know it's a good initiative. It deserves to succeed. They are helping the government. Minnesota could lose billions if this project stalls. Not to mention the adverse publicity that might cloud it forevermore if it's not solved fast. Please, just see it from the other side," he encouraged his stubborn friend.

The governor sighed.

Timms could see he was thinking hard. His argument had made an impact. But he wasn't backing down. From the way he was narrowing his eyes, Timms knew with a flare of dread that he was simply thinking up a better way of maneuvering.

"Okay," he said at last. "If these guys are worth what you say, and they're as good as you say, then they need to be faster than the police would be."

"They are," Timms insisted.

"I know the average solve time for the police. So, to better that time, this task force needs to solve this today. If they can catch the killer before sundown tonight, and get this operation back on track, then I acknowledge they have real value and I will back off and let them be. In fact, I'm prepared to let them have autonomy in the future. Complete autonomy as a unit." He sounded proud, as if he was making a generous offer.

"But," Timms began, feeling panic surge, because this was all but impossible. The governor silenced him with a look.

"If they don't solve this to my satisfaction by nightfall, then the police might as well be on this, and it proves that the task force does not add real value. So in that case, it's a no. No argument, no negotiation. A no."

Timms capitulated. There was no sense in fighting further, and if he did, the governor was capable of withdrawing this final condition that was the only hope they had.

"I appreciate that you're giving it a chance," he said. He was trying to remain polite. This was a typical tactic from this man. He'd give you what you wanted and more – but make the conditions impossible. Then it was your fault that you failed.

There could be no going back, because in the corner, the assistant was already busy with the minutes of the meeting, which Timms knew would be in his inbox by the time he got back to the office. Everything in writing, signed, and sealed.

And most probably undeliverable.

He stood up, feeling deeply conflicted.

The challenge had been made, the gauntlet had been thrown down.

The survival of the task force now rested on a knife edge that was far beyond anyone's control.

If Katie and her partner solved the crime in time, they would stay. And if not, they were gone. It was a shockingly short timeframe in which to solve a case with such scanty evidence.

An impossible timeframe, realistically speaking.

Timms knew with a cold certainty that the governor would keep his word. And that he fully expected them to fail.

CHAPTER SEVENTEEN

As Katie and Leblanc climbed into their rental SUV, Katie was still feeling deeply shocked at what she had seen. Something about the vulnerability of that body, cradled in the tree, made her feel viscerally disturbed and even more determined to find out who was responsible. Widening the net was the next logical move, since the construction site itself seemed well managed, with no opportunity for a rogue killer from those crews to roam and strike.

Because the kills had started so recently, it was surely logical that another crew, working nearby, might be responsible. If not, they would then have to investigate people with a motive in the town itself. But Katie thought that given the speed and suddenness of these kills, it could well be that the killer was from a neighboring crew, someone who had recently arrived, who was living out their murderous urges, believing they were anonymous and would never be found.

They headed out of the site in silence. It was a cool, breezy morning. A weak sun was struggling to break through low clouds, but only a few brighter glimpses were yet visible.

"If we don't find anyone working nearby, then the town itself can be our next step," Katie suggested.

Leblanc shook his head. "I think it's someone who has recently arrived here. I believe we are looking for a bad apple, someone who is using the circumstances to kill, knowing that this place is full of temporary workers."

At least they had options, Katie thought, trying to see the situation in a positive light, even though she felt their best leads hadn't panned out, and had the uneasy feeling they were already clutching at straws.

"True," she agreed.

They started up the SUV and drove over the rutted track, heading out of the construction site. Katie noticed that there were several people at the entrance looking stressed and worried. They seemed to be setting up a boom gate system.

She knew it wouldn't help and she knew they knew too. But in that situation, it was at least some kind of action that they could take. She understood only too well how ineffectual they felt. So did she.

77

They drove in silence for a while, passing a convoy of trucks heading toward the construction site.

"Turn right here. This might take us around the site," Katie suggested, doing her best to get her bearings in this thickly forested area.

Leblanc did as she suggested.

They drove over a humpback bridge, which was a few yards above a creek. Past the bridge, the road began to climb.

"What's that on the right?" Katie had spotted a few roofs, hidden in the trees.

Leblanc drove closer. They stopped and climbed out.

The air smelled different here, away from the diesel and dust of the construction site. She could pick up the smell of pine, the freshness of the breeze.

"It's a campsite," Leblanc said, as they walked down the overgrown path. "But it looks to be disused."

"Yes, it does."

The simple, basic buildings looked neat and tidy, but the grass was long and the windows were dirty.

"Perhaps it gets used in summer," Katie wondered. "It's still early in the season for a family to go camping. Still cold and rainy."

"Yes. That must be it. It doesn't look occupied at all."

Katie felt disappointed as this would have been a good hideout for a killer.

But then, she saw something beyond, in the valley.

"Leblanc, look there. There are people at work down there. It looks like they are setting up power lines."

The activity was barely discernible through the trees.

"So they are," Leblanc said. "Let's drive around and get closer. If they are running power lines through to the new development, then we definitely need to investigate them."

Katie felt motivated as she got back into the car. She was glad their detour to the campsite had allowed her to spot the power lines.

They climbed back in the car and headed out again. A short while later they reached a track heading in the direction of the power lines.

This was more promising. If the bad apple theory was correct, then the person responsible for the crimes might just be among the crew working on the power lines. That would make sense.

The SUV bounced along the track, slowly making progress.

Katie noticed that a narrow row of trees had been cut down for as far as she could see in either direction.

"This must be where the power lines are going to run," she said. They must be cutting down trees and clearing the area. I think it's a good place to start, checking the people working there."

As the car approached, they could see that a temporary camp, consisting of tents, a portable toilet, and a few vehicles, was located in the trees. In contrast with the site clearing, this activity was much quieter. But Katie was impressed by how tall the power lines were. These were large steel structures, more than thirty feet high, capable of carrying serious voltage. As she watched, one of the workers shimmied up the structure, carrying a line of cable with him.

"They sure do need to be able to climb in this job," Leblanc said meaningfully.

"Yes," Katie agreed. She felt as if this was an important observation. Among this crew might just be the opportunistic, skilled killer they were seeking.

There were about ten people working on and around the power lines. When they stopped the car, one of the men walked over immediately. He looked to be in his thirties, wearing a hard hat, a reflective jacket, and an ID tag that identified him as Raymond Flannery from City Power.

"Can I help you?" he asked.

"I hope so. We are detectives and we are investigating a series of murders that have recently occurred in this area, specifically at the construction site nearby," Katie said.

Flannery nodded. "That's very troubling. I've heard about it, of course. Why are you here?"

"We're wondering if you've seen anything out of the ordinary," Katie said. "Anyone watching your site, lurking around. Or if you've had any problems with any of your workers. A trouble causer, anyone who has a criminal record, maybe even someone you fired recently."

Flannery frowned thoughtfully. "There was an incident involving our crew. I don't know if it would be helpful to you."

"Please, tell us," Leblanc said.

"We did have a problem employee on site. He got into an argument with the shift boss a few days ago, when we were still working further north. He actually ended up trying to push him off one of the pylons. That's very dangerous behavior. He could have killed him."

Katie felt a flare of excitement. This was sounding as if it was getting somewhere.

"Who's the employee?" she asked.

"His name's John Tait. He was a local guy that we hired a couple of weeks ago."

"And where is he now?"

"We suspended him immediately without pay."

"And how did he respond to that?"

The boss man sighed. "The same way he's responded to everything so far. Badly. Abusive, threatening, and trying to get physically violent."

"What did you do?"

"We removed him from site immediately and banned him from coming back. We don't allow dangerous behavior. We work with electrical power at height. We simply can't afford anyone like that to be on site at all. The full disciplinary process still needs to take place, and without a doubt he'll be fired, but for now, I guess he's back at his home address in the town. We had to chase him away a few times. He lurked around site for a while. Climbed trees, and shouted threats at us, said we hadn't heard the last of him."

Katie felt encouraged that this suspect was actually a local, and he'd been working on a related construction project. The timeline of the trouble he'd gotten into fit in with the start of the killing spree, and he was a violent man who had a reason to be angry and had clearly been looking for ways to vent his rage.

Finally, it seemed they were making progress.

"Please, can you give me his address?" she said. "We need to go to his house and speak to him, right now."

CHAPTER EIGHTEEN

John Tait lived at number four Kestrel Drive, and Katie felt a sense of impatience as they approached the quiet road, winding into the hills on the far side of the small town of Ashton.

John's circumstances and behavior had raised so many red flags that she couldn't wait to get face-to-face with him.

Was this the man they were looking for, and had they been so close to him all along?

"There it is. Number four," Leblanc said, slowing to a halt.

Katie jumped out, and she and Leblanc hurried up the path. Katie saw that this home was neat and well kept. It was a small, humble, wooden house. Roses were planted in large pots on either side of the front door. They were just beginning to bud.

She pressed the bell, and a muffled, insistent ringing came from inside.

She heard movement, and after a few moments, a face appeared, peering through the glass.

It was a blonde woman, who looked to be in her late twenties. She was holding a purse in her hand and had a jacket slung over her shoulder, which made Katie think she was about to leave for work.

She seemed surprised to see them there.

"Good morning," she said hesitantly, opening the door.

"Good morning," Katie said. "We're police. We're investigating the murders that have been taking place in and near the construction site."

A frown appeared on her face. "I'm Sharon Edgar. Yes, I heard about those, but I'm not sure how I can help you. I work for the town's tourism board, and everyone is very concerned about this, but I haven't had anything to do with the construction site."

"We're actually looking for John Tait," Katie said. "We need to get some information from him."

"John? He's not here. He hasn't been here for a few days now. He stays with me usually; he's my boyfriend. Sort of," Sharon amended. "A sort of boyfriend. But he's gotten a job working on the power line construction."

Katie raised her eyebrows inwardly. It was clear that Sharon had no idea of the recent events that had played out.

"Has he been in contact with you at all in the past few days?" she asked.

"No, not since he left for site."

Now Katie was starting to feel anxious. They needed to locate this man! Where was he?

"Does he have any other relatives here? Any friends he stays with, or has stayed with?"

She shook her head. "No, only me. He's been staying with me for about a year now. He moved in as a lodger when his aunt moved out of town. Then he became a boyfriend. Kind of."

Katie was getting the strong impression that John Tait did not specialize in good relationships, generally. But where else in town could he logically be? Or was he still hiding out in the woods. That was also a scenario they had to look at.

"Has he called you?"

"No. He texted me once or twice, but not for a couple of days."

She twined her fingers together, looking unhappy at this line of questioning.

"Can you give me his number?" Katie asked.

Sharon read it out. "I'm not sure how much help it will be, because I've called him a couple of times in the past two days and his phone's been turned off," she said.

"It's good to have it anyway," Katie said.

"Is he in trouble?" she asked.

"We just want to speak with him about a matter that might be related to the case, but we're not sure where he is."

"All I know is that he's on site. He took his clothes and some other gear with him, enough for a week or two," she said apologetically. "I'm afraid I don't know anything that might help you to find him," she said. "He can be a bit of a difficult person sometimes, but he's never been violent."

She paused, then she said, "I hope he's not in some kind of trouble. He's never caused me any trouble."

"If there is anything you need to know, we will tell you," Katie said. "For now, we'll do our best to locate him. What does he look like? Do you have a photo?"

"Sure. This is what he looks like. He's quite a slim guy, fit, and about five-ten in height."

She opened her phone to show Katie a photo of an unsmiling man with a strong jaw and blonde, buzz-cut hair.

"Okay. Thank you."

The woman gave them a final apologetic smile before locking the door and hurrying out to the small garage. A moment later, she drove off.

Katie felt a sense of urgency as they hurried back to their own car. Where in this small town could he be? What was he doing?

"We need to find out where he is. He's the most likely suspect for these murders so far. His behavior is too extreme to ignore. What if he snapped?"

Leblanc looked thoughtful. "Katie, when he snapped, he might have decided to start the killings. That's the kind of person he sounds like."

Katie stopped in her tracks, turning to Leblanc, feeling excited.

"That's exactly the kind of person he is. The kind of person who would want to vent his rage. He could have tipped over into murdering people on or near the main site to begin with. But he might also be somewhere nearby where the power line crews are. Keeping them in his sights. Planning something for them."

Leblanc narrowed his eyes. "They said that they started further north. Shall we see if we can pick up where these power lines started, and then find out if John Tait is anywhere nearby?"

They climbed into the car and drove out of town. Katie was starting to get her bearings now. She was getting more of a feel for the pattern of what was happening. The town itself was nestled in a fold of the hills, among the woods. The construction was on a sloping plain to the north. The power lines would therefore have started at a point to the north, and be running south in the direction of town.

Leblanc drove along the temporary track, and both he and Katie stared around, searching for the point where the work had started.

"There," Katie said, pointing. "That has to be it."

She could see old tire marks in the mud, which must have been left by the construction vehicles. There were large, yellow metal poles that supported the power lines, and a small, metal, white-painted cabin.

There was no sign of life anywhere near the original site. The two of them climbed out and walked closer, and Katie looked around carefully.

"No recent footprints. No sign of anyone being here. They put these pylons up and they moved on."

"So now, we follow the pylons, and keep a lookout for anyone nearby, any sign of a tent in the woods, any evidence of sabotage."

Katie hoped her hunch was correct. It felt like an insurmountable challenge to find this man. It felt like a needle in a haystack. But she felt it was likely, based on what she had learned about his personality so far, that he would not have scattered to the winds, and might be here, causing further trouble.

They climbed back into the car and drove on, following the route of the power lines. The sky was brightening, and it was nearly noon.

"There's someone up there, working on one of the pylons," Katie said, spotting a tiny figure, high up on one of the shiny, new steel structures. "Shall we ask him?"

"I guess we could, but isn't it a waste of time to ask everyone we meet?" Leblanc said. Katie could tell he was also becoming discouraged with the vastness of this search. "Shouldn't we track this guy's phone?"

"We can do that, for sure, if it's turned on, but Sharon said it was off," Katie said. "Shall we check this guy out, and then call Scott and ask him to get us a location if it's available?"

Leblanc shrugged morosely. He drove down the rutted track until they reached the pylon.

"So what are we going to ask this lonely man?" he challenged her.

But something about the scene was setting off alarm bells for Katie.

"A man on his own? Leblanc, I don't think this is a worker. He's not even wearing a helmet. This is him! Look at that hair, it's blonde for sure. It's him. And he's not up here working. That's why he's on his own."

Now, at last, Leblanc had overcome his sour mood and looked as excited as Katie felt.

"He's sabotaging the lines. He must be! And we can get him now. We can catch him in the act."

Katie scrambled out of the car and hurried over to the pylon.

"John Tait?" she called. "What are you doing up there? Are you authorized to be there? We need to speak to you."

The man high above her froze.

He turned and stared down at her. It was difficult to see him, with the sun now shining brightly behind him.

He lashed out his arm. And a moment later, she heard Leblanc's urgent cry.

"Katie! Move, quick!"

He grabbed her arm and tugged her out of the way.

With a clanging noise, a heavy spanner ricocheted through the air, narrowly missing Katie's shoulder.

It thudded to the ground and she gasped with shock. Leblanc had pulled her out of the path of what could have been a lethal weapon.

This was John Tait. No doubt about it.

He'd seen they were police and that they were targeting him. And now, he was on the attack.

CHAPTER NINETEEN

"Katie, move out of range!" Leblanc's voice was urgent, thrumming with tension. But Katie had other ideas. No way was she allowing a suspect to get away with this.

"John Tait, come down. We need to speak to you," she called firmly.

There was no response. Silhouetted against the shimmering sun, the figure was unmoving.

"We need a ladder," Leblanc muttered.

"A ladder will take time to organize," she said to Leblanc. "And if we leave here, it gives him the chance to run."

She could see Leblanc was anxious for her. But she didn't care. Some things had to be risked.

"Alright," Katie said mostly to herself. "I'm going to come up and get you, then."

Ignoring Leblanc's warning cry, she put a hand onto the steel pylon.

The metal felt solid, and surprisingly cold under her hand. The structure stretched above her, high into the sky. But she needed to do this. There was no time to waste. They could be there for hours, otherwise, and this case couldn't wait. Not when this killer was grabbing anyone he could, whose height and weight were within the physical limits of what he could carry to his treetop tombs.

Katie put her foot on the pylon and began to climb.

She could hear Leblanc shouting warnings at her from below. He sounded furious at what she was doing. But she had to do this. She needed to confront this man, to take him on, and to find out if he was the one terrorizing this site.

The climb was harder than she had imagined. The pylon was slippery, and she had to grip the metal tightly with both hands.

She felt the roughness of the steel under her hands, and the cold of it bit into her flesh. As she climbed, the cold air was whipping around her, and the metal surface was slippery under her boots.

Her hands were slick with sweat as she tried to find a better hold.

"Katie, come down!" Leblanc sounded scared, too. But she couldn't turn back. She had to get to this man, face-to-face with him. She had to show him she was not afraid.

Up here, the wind was much stronger. It tugged at her, trying to take her over the side. She felt a small but definite vibration in the steel structure, as if it was a living thing, sensing her.

She heard a heartfelt curse from below her. And then, the structure vibrated and rattled as Leblanc began to climb. He was joining her up here, in the air; he was coming up the other side of the pylon, which meant that Tait was effectively trapped.

She reached out again, and pulled herself higher.

She climbed on, upward toward him, her heart thudding in her chest.

I can do this, she told herself firmly. I'm a professional. I must do my job, with purpose, and without fear.

But she couldn't help a flash of fear at how high she was.

Don't think of falling, she warned herself, as a brief rush of dizziness made her sway for a moment. She climbed onto the next level of the pylon, and clambered up. Now she was much higher. The sun was dazzling her. She didn't dare to look down. But still, she climbed on.

"John Tait, we need to speak to you," she called.

"Go away. What the hell are you doing up here?"

It was the first words he'd spoken. His voice was rough, and she realized he sounded scared, too.

"We need to speak to you," Katie insisted.

"I'm doing maintenance work, nothing wrong with that. Leave me be."

"You're not doing maintenance work. You were suspended from the crew. My guess is you're interfering with the wiring here; you're looking to sabotage this. I want to know what else you've been trying to sabotage. What else you've done in the past few days."

Now she was on a level with him, clinging to the steel structure. Behind her, Leblanc, looking sheet-pale, was hanging onto the steel bars as if for grim death. But they were there, and they had him bracketed.

He stared from one of them to the other. He frowned.

And then, letting go the structure with one hand, he lunged for Katie.

87

She couldn't help it. She cried out in shock as his hand lashed out at her. She clung to the railing, kicking reflexively out at him, regretting the action immediately as her other foot nearly slipped off the slick, sloping tread of steel.

Behind her, Leblanc swore again. He clambered closer. Glancing at him, she saw a sheen of perspiration covered his face.

Katie hung on for grim death. Tait was trying to dislodge her, to get her hand off the pylon, he was lashing out at her fingers. If he caught her hand, she didn't want to think about what might happen. Her footing up here was precarious. They must be forty feet in the air. Without a doubt, she'd plummet down to death or serious injury.

She moved her hand, gasping as he lashed at her again.

Bracing herself to resist this attack, Katie flailed desperately around, looking to find a better purchase, and not thinking about what a loss of balance would mean.

"Stop it!" Leblanc harangued the man from behind, tension thrumming in his voice. "This is attempted murder. Every action you are taking here. You are going to get jail time. Stop it!"

Leblanc must have summoned up all his courage to make the move, but he made it. With a sudden fast action, his hand flicked out. He caught Tait by the shoulders and this time, to Katie's amazement, Leblanc held him. His hand gripped the man's jacket, and he pulled him back.

With a sharp cry of terror, Tait now had his grasp on the metal loosened.

Seeing her chance, Katie made a grab for his flailing hand. She wedged her elbow around the steel, summoned all her courage, and hung on as hard as she could.

With his feet wedged in place, his face intense and focused, Leblanc maneuvered closer. He got a pair of handcuffs off his belt. Tait was twisting and writhing, trying to get away, but he couldn't, because he needed one hand to hold himself in place, and Katie had the other. He was pinned between them, high in the air, and the only possible escape for him now was a lethal fall.

Leblanc clipped one of the cuffs onto the man's wrist. Tait cried out in alarm, but he couldn't move the wrist. He was breathing fast. Panting in fear.

Katie found a grip on the steel frame and clambered toward him.

The wind buffeted her, nearly knocking her off balance. His free hand whipped out again, and this time she managed to block it, twisting his fingers back without losing her footing.

She heard a howl of rage as he tried to clutch his injured hand to his chest.

He swayed again, nearly losing his balance.

"Alright, alright," he gasped breathlessly. "You - you're gonna kill me. I'll come down. I'm not going to try and escape."

"I don't trust you. I'm keeping hold of this handcuff," Leblanc threatened him. His voice was ragged with fear, but resolute nonetheless.

"And I'm climbing in front of you," Katie added. "Follow me down. Slow. No struggling. You're already in a world of trouble. Don't make it worse."

In what was surely the most bizarre arrest of a suspect she'd ever made, she began the stomach-churning journey back to the ground.

It had been risky and dangerous, but they finally had their suspect cuffed and subdued.

As soon as they were on solid ground, Katie was ready to question him about his involvement in the murders.

CHAPTER TWENTY

Katie felt a rush of relief as her feet hit the uneven earth below the pylon, and she was able to let go of the cold, clanging steel. She turned immediately back to the other two men above her, because this was a dangerous part of the operation. When Tait reached ground level, he might try to break away from Leblanc's grasp. They couldn't risk him fleeing, and nor could they risk him pulling Leblanc off the pylon when he was still high enough to risk serious injury.

As soon as he was within reach, Katie grabbed Tait's arm again. She clipped her own handcuffs on. Now, they each had a pair of handcuffs attached to the man.

But it was clear that the fight had gone out of Tait. He was sweating visibly as his feet hit the ground. He was breathing hard. He flinched as Katie yanked his hand behind his back, securing the other cuff as Leblanc let go on his side for the final leap down.

"You're in deep trouble," she threatened him. "That was a criminal action up there. What were you thinking? Are you a criminal, Tait?"

"Is that what this is about?" He was looking pale and horrified. "You're arresting me for this sabotage? I swear, I did nothing. You can check. The wires are still there."

"It's not about the sabotage." Katie thought again what a strange location this was for a suspect interview. In a rutted, newly dug power line servitude, with the man backed up against the cold steel, under the cold, glimmering eye of a spring midday sun.

"What's it about then?"

"The murders."

Tait frowned. "Murders? I don't know what you mean. Who's been murdered?"

Katie wasn't letting him get away with a plea of ignorance.

"You need to account for your movements over the past couple of days. Specifically, in the small hours of this morning. At about four a.m."

If he had an alibi for the most recent murder, then it cleared him, she knew. If he didn't, then she would work back, but last night's murder was the most accurate timeline they had to work with.

She didn't think he would be cleared. He looked panicked and guilty and afraid. Up there, he'd clearly felt invulnerable and had been - literally - on a high of confidence.

Now, down on the raw soil, reality was kicking in. She could see he was beginning to panic. He was shaking his head.

"I - I don't know," he muttered. "I can't say."

"If you're innocent, you have nothing to worry about," she said to him. "I need to hear your account of what you've been doing."

"Tell us!" Leblanc ordered, walking around to stand over him threateningly. "You're in a lot of trouble already. Unless you want to face certain jail time, you'd better answer."

Tait stared from one of them to the other. He looked completely trapped.

Katie felt a flare of triumph. This was it, they had their suspect, and he had no alibi because he was the killer.

But then, in a stilted and stammering voice, he began to speak.

"Look, you're right. I was suspended from the site. They probably blamed me for it but I can tell you they were at fault, too. I'm the one who got punished," he ranted.

Katie waited for some semblance of fact to be discernible amid this blustering.

"I didn't go back home. I didn't want Sharon to know, I mean, I didn't want to have to tell her. So I went and stayed with a friend over in the next town. He picked me up. I can show you our entire conversation. I called him and told him and he came and fetched me because I don't have a car. Last night, we went out to a bar. We got back at about one in the morning, I think, and we both turned in. He had to leave for work at six a.m. so we were up again at five. We stopped and got breakfast. I paid for that, and asked him to drop me near here for the day."

"Show me the evidence," Katie said firmly.

"It - it's all here. I - here's the messages. Here's our conversation. Look, you can see. And it's his car. I mean, I wouldn't take his car. I couldn't. It was locked in the garage overnight, with the alarm on."

He handed his phone over.

Katie was not going to let one detail slip past her and she was very aware that a fake alibi could have been created for just this eventuality.

She scrolled from app to app, checking and double checking.

She didn't see a false note, though.

91

From the angry text asking his friend to come and fetch him, to the bar photos from last night and the notification of the electronic payment he'd made at a diner fifty miles to the west of here at six-thirty a.m., the version he was giving them was true.

And Katie had to admit it was also plausible. His bruised ego had not allowed him to go back to his 'sort of' girlfriend and explain the truth. Instead, he'd run off and licked his wounds, before regrouping and attempting petty damage.

There was still the matter of having attempted to assault her by throwing the spanner down at her. And Katie felt ready to pursue those charges. Tait deserved nothing less.

But at that moment, her phone rang.

It was Scott, and she felt her stomach clench, because she thought for sure there must have been another victim found.

"Watch him," she said to Leblanc, before hurrying away, out of earshot, to take the call.

"Katie." Her boss's voice resonated with stress. "Any progress?"

"We just got a suspect, but his alibi checked out," she admitted.

Scott sighed. There was a level of tension in his voice she'd never picked up before in her usually calm boss.

"We have a serious situation here. You could even call it a critical situation," he explained.

"What - what's happening?" she asked.

"The future of the task force. Someone, high up, has done a deal or made an agreement with someone else. I'm not going to give you the names. Those are not going to be helpful right now. What's helpful to us are the facts. The facts, documented and in black and white in front of me, are that if we solve this case before sundown tonight, the unit will remain as is, with full autonomy in the future. But if this case is not solved, then it is dissolved. It's the end for us."

Katie gasped.

The pressure felt like a lead weight, bearing down. Never had she thought they could be in a more precarious situation than they had been fifteen minutes ago, in the cold, breezy air atop that pylon.

But this felt worse. This felt as if the ground had been yanked all the way from under her.

"How is that even possible? What kind of deal has been struck?" As reality sunk in, she added, "That's hugely unfair. In a way, that's like setting us up for failure. Why should the unit's future depend on this? What about all our other successes?"

"I don't know. I agree it's unfair. I agree with what you have said. We are being trapped in a political situation that is undoubtedly being created to destroy us, while using a seemingly reasonable deadline that we all know is not achievable."

"Exactly. You can't put a timeframe on this! There are only two of us, it's a huge area, there's a massive field of potential suspects and directions still to uncover."

Scott's sigh told her that her words were futile.

"We don't have a choice. This is the situation. This is our only get-out-of-jail card, if you like to think of it that way. Our only chance. We have to take it, or else, the unit ceases to exist. And that's why I want you to do whatever you can, whatever you have to. By sundown, Katie."

"I'll do my best," she said woodenly.

Scott disconnected with a click.

Katie's mind was churning. This put the whole investigation into a different gear.

Already, it was after one p.m. The sun would set at seven-thirty p.m., give or take a few minutes.

That was all the time they had.

Just six short hours stood between them and their task force's certain destruction.

CHAPTER TWENTY ONE

Katie walked back to where Leblanc was standing with Tait. In an ideal world they would press charges, take him in, make sure he was punished for his aggressive, irresponsible actions.

But they had no time now. As much as it burned her, she was going to have to put his misdemeanors aside, and focus on what they needed to do to survive. At least she knew that the electrical crew would follow up on his actions, and retribution would come from that side.

"You can go," she said briefly.

Tait's eyes widened as if he could not believe his luck.

"I can?" he asked, still not quite believing it. "You're - you're not going to take me in?"

She shook her head.

"No. We're handling a murder case. We don't have time to focus on you. It does not mean your actions will not have consequences. You need to seriously think about what you've been doing. Because it won't be me that gets you next time. But it will be someone else. You're on a destructive path. You should serve jail time for what you did up there. And next time, you will."

He nodded emptily. "Thanks. I guess I needed to hear that. I'm sorry, I apologize. I didn't - well, I'm glad you're letting me off. I'll rethink my behavior. You're right. There's a lot to change."

He turned and walked away, trailing his feet, heading in the direction of the main road a few hundred yards away.

Katie and Leblanc watched him go.

Leblanc was the first to speak. He didn't say anything immediately. Only when Tait was about fifty yards away, and out of earshot, did Leblanc let rip.

"What the hell was that about?" he yelled at Katie.

"What?" Katie stared at him feeling totally confused. "The phone call? It was Scott. I had to take it."

"Not the phone call!" Leblanc was furious. Katie could now feel the anger emanating from him. "Not the phone call! Climbing up that structure to get to Tait! You could have fallen! You could have died!"

"I didn't think about it at the time," she admitted. "But I didn't. I'm standing here, healthy. No harm done. And it was the only way to get to the top, so I had to do it."

"It was a crazy, unnecessary risk. A totally insane choice. It's one thing to take risks to get information from a suspect," Leblanc told her, his face tightening up into a scowl. "It's another thing entirely to take risks to get information from a suspect who is already showing signs of aggression! At height. Without any safety equipment or attachments preventing you from falling."

"I didn't think about it," she repeated.

"That's not good enough!" Leblanc was practically yelling now.

"It's my job," Katie said, feeling her own anger rising. "My job involves risks."

"Not insane ones! You could have died," Leblanc said again, his voice stronger.

"I'm fine! I don't need you to control me. You did what you had to do. Supported me."

"I could have lost you!" he yelled.

"You didn't!" she yelled back.

And then they stopped, because they heard the words they were fighting over, the words they had not said.

Leblanc had been there for her. She realized now that he was scared of heights, more than she. And yet, he'd gone up there. Conquered his fear, been by her side. If he had not been there, they would not have achieved this. On her own, Katie acknowledged, things could have gone very differently.

"I'm sorry," she said. It was difficult for her to apologize. She hated backing down on decisions she had made. That did not come easy for her, not at all. But she knew that Leblanc deserved it. "I agree. It was wrong of me, and it was too reckless."

He was still seething, though.

"It's unacceptable," he ranted. "And to make it worse, now you let this guy go? What for? Are we just giving free passes here? Why are you acting this way?"

Katie had to cut it short. There was no time for a fight.

"Scott called," she snapped.

"And? What did he say?" Leblanc's wrath had abated. She saw that immediately. He sensed her tone.

"We're in an impossible situation."

Now that she'd coped with Leblanc's anger, Katie herself was starting to acknowledge the enormity of the unfair terms they had been hit with. She felt as if she was reeling with shock all over again as she thought about them.

"Impossible how?"

"There - there are people up top. Maneuvering politically. They've given us a deadline that we won't be able to meet, to solve this case. It's being done to try and make out like we had a chance, before they shut down the unit."

"What?" Now Leblanc sounded incredulous.

"We have till sunset. That's it. Sunset. After that, the unit is gone. Disbanded. And it will be our fault, because the person making these decisions, who is a state governor, gave us this case to prove ourselves and we failed."

Leblanc blinked fast.

"Katie, this can't be right. Are you serious?"

"I am. And it isn't right but it's the kind of thing they do. Making an impossible decision seem reasonable when they know that the outcome will serve their agenda. They can say - well, the average police time to solve a case is 'X' hours. Look, we have stats to prove it. And we gave the unit one final chance and they didn't do it appreciably faster than 'X' hours, so we can conclude they are dispensable."

"I don't believe this."

"It's what we are up against. But we do have a chance. And we're lucky we do. Leblanc, someone worked hard to give us this chance. This window of opportunity. For it to be there at all is a miracle. If we solve this by sunset, we have it in black and white that the unit will survive. There is absolutely no doubt, and there can be no further argument against it."

She stared at him and saw her own fear reflected in his eyes. What this all meant to them. To her and Leblanc. To their future, their career. The team they respected so deeply. And their relationship.

He nodded. "Now I understand why you let him go, because there isn't time to do anything else."

"There isn't. We have to focus on this."

She knew he shared all her deepest fears. The fear of failure. The fear of unfair consequences. The fear of never seeing each other again, and having to end this fulfilling direction of their careers.

For just a second, Katie saw the fear in his eyes too. In spite of his bravado. He knew what it meant to her, because it meant the same to him.

"Where do we go next?" he asked.

"I guess we have to continue where we were headed," Katie said. "We need to go into town. We can't divert our line of thinking. It's the only one we have. The only one there is. We still have to work out who had the ability and the motive to get into this construction site, and the surrounding area. It wasn't anyone on site that we can find. It wasn't the power line workers. That leaves the town residents, and anyone with a grudge against the development. Someone who has something to lose."

"Okay," he agreed. "So we do what we were planning, but faster."

She gave him a reluctant grin. "That's it. The same, but faster."

Focusing on the humor made it easier to ignore the ramifications of the consequences.

"We're going to go to town. Then what?"

"In a small town, apart from the gossip grapevine, there are two main places that would have information that we need. The local media, and the local police department. Between them, they would be very well connected to all of the trouble and the negative sentiment that this development could have generated."

"You are right. Those would be the two main focus points. Do we go together?"

"Time is against us. Let's each take one," Katie suggested. "You take the police department. I'll go find the media. Let's touch base as soon as we've spoken to them and see if we can uncover any evidence of anyone with a grudge or a motive who's from this town."

CHAPTER TWENTY TWO

"The media" was a grand term for the tiny apartment where the local journalist lived. Having called the main office of the county's website and paper, Katie had discovered that Ashton was too small to have its own local publication. It was included in the wider area's media circulation, but it had its own on-site reporter.

Her name was Simone Ellingworth and she lived in the north of town. The apartment was above a restaurant and coffee shop.

Katie walked up the narrow staircase, only to find a notice there.

"Working at Movida."

That was the coffee shop. She hurried down the stairs again, and pushed open the door to the small, cozy, coffee-scented space.

She spotted Simone immediately. She was dark-haired, pretty, looked to be in her thirties, and had a laptop and phone set up at a corner table where she was on a call, speaking with a serious look on her face. Probably working on the murder story, Katie thought.

Nodding a greeting to the white-uniformed barista at the counter, Katie walked over and waited until Simone had finished the call.

"Can I speak to you for a moment, Ms. Ellingworth?" she asked.

Simone gave her a knowing look. "You're police? Sure. Is this about the murders?"

"It is," Katie agreed.

"It's such a terrible situation. It's my first murder case, and I've been working for the North Minnesota News, which covers all the towns in this area, for four years now."

"I'm hoping you can help us with your local knowledge."

"I don't know what I can do, but I'm happy to answer any questions," Simone said doubtfully.

"As the local media, you would receive all the complaints about the development from people in this town who wanted them publicized? Is that right?"

Simone nodded. "Sure. Yes, there have been some people who have approached me."

"Who are the ones who've been the angriest about it?" Katie asked. She was looking to pinpoint the strongest motive.

"There have been a lot of complaints about noise, especially when they started clearing the site, working closest to town," Simone said thoughtfully. "Some of those were vociferous."

"That would be a big factor. Are there other biggies?"

Simone brightened. "There is the loss of habitat. A lot of people own land around here which they use for hunting and fishing. I had a few complaints from land owners who worried this development will either restrict or damage both, because of the increased population. A few letters to the editor, pleas for action or protection."

Katie didn't quite feel she was getting what she needed.

"Has anyone reacted aggressively? With threats, anything like that?"

"In this town?" Simone thought carefully.

"Yes," Katie said.

After a minute, Simone spoke again.

"One of the local birders. He runs a tour operation taking people on birding walks. He was very unpleasant about it at one stage."

The birding connection was interesting. Perhaps that was a message being sent, Katie thought. Those bodies up in trees had been reminiscent of nests. Was the idea to illustrate to the local community that this was what would happen to the habitat?

"What's his name?" Katie asked.

She looked at her notes. "Brian Banner."

"Has any of his communication been aggressive?" Katie asked, wanting to get a feel for how Brian Banner was approaching the situation.

"Very," Simone agreed. "His communication is all aggressive. We've been unable to publish it. The North Minnesota News actually had to send him a legal letter to tell him to stop threatening me, personally."

"He did that?" Katie asked, surprised.

"Yes, because we wouldn't publish his threats. We couldn't. They were threats. They were based on exaggerated and incorrect information. He threatened to put a spoke in the operations and that people who were on or near the site should watch out. He threatened to get me fired and claimed that I was incapable. And he then blamed me for killing the story, as he put it. He called me several times a day. He even arrived here, at the coffee shop, but the owner locked him out when he saw him. It's one of the advantages to working here. At least there are people around."

"I'm sorry to hear that he's been behaving this way." The more Katie was hearing about this man, the more she realized he was a loose cannon who'd had a direct issue with the construction. He could have had a psychotic break, and begun killing anyone he perceived as being close to the site.

"For sure, he's a trouble causer. I know he's a local businessman and he feels his interests are going to be affected, although I don't think it is necessarily true. But there are ways of doing things, and the way he chose doesn't reflect well on him, or his business. Threats, swearing, more threats. I must say at one time I felt unsafe."

"And he lives in town?"

"He does, yes."

Katie felt as if she was getting closer to the killer. Much closer. They had a birding guide mad at the development. One who had the personality and character that defaulted toward aggression. He had threatened the woman personally. He had threatened the media. What had happened next?

"I appreciate you telling me this," Katie said.

"He's the only person from this town I've had those problems with. But it only takes one to make the job difficult," Simone acknowledged.

Only one. That meant Katie's job was simple.

She needed to go and confront the aggressive birder. She would have preferred to do so with Leblanc. But with time being so tight, and this lead being local, she decided it would make sense to go without him.

"Do you have any idea where I can find him?"

Simone nodded. "I've no idea where he lives, but his business is at the end of First Street. There's a large sign outside. 'The Bird Watcher's Guide.' You can't miss it."

Katie decided to head straight there, in the likelihood that the birder would be at work. If he wasn't, she knew that Scott could give her his home address within a few minutes.

The town was so small that First Street was just a two-minute walk away. Katie hurried down the street, looking for the sign that she'd been told about.

She spotted it on a small white building. *The Bird Watcher's Guide.*

It was a single-story building, with the signage on the street and the door on the side. Katie walked up the few steps and into the compact office.

There were photos of birds on the walls. Maps and books lined the shelves. Binoculars, caps, and other items were stacked at the small desk in the musty-smelling room.

An elderly lady sat behind the desk. Quickly, Katie approached her.

"I'm looking for Mr. Brian Banner. Is he in?"

She shook her head. "He went out on a walking tour with a customer about ten minutes ago."

So she'd just missed him. That was frustrating.

"Do you know if he took a specific route?"

"Oh, yes," the elderly lady said. "He was going to head down to the lake. If you go down to the end of the road, you'll see the trail. He had a young woman with him. He said they might be a while, and that she might go on for a solo hike, I believe."

Katie felt anxiety flare. At this time, heading out alone with a young woman represented all sorts of risk. Sending her on a solo hike was sounding risky. It was sounding as if he was setting her up to disappear.

Would he be looking to kill a paying client? Katie wasn't sure, but she knew, with a chill, that the behavior of psychopaths could easily escalate. Having done three successful murders, he could now be looking to add to the numbers, using the solo hike as the excuse.

"I'll go and catch up with them now," she said.

She rushed out of the office, and headed for the trail at a run.

CHAPTER TWENTY THREE

Leblanc walked up the stairs of the local police department as Katie drove off. He hoped that his time here would be productive and that by the end of this visit, he would have identified a suspect.

"Good morning," he greeted the sergeant. "Detective Leblanc, from the task force investigating the murders. I would like to check your records. We're looking for anyone who might have caused trouble at the construction site in the past weeks. Anyone whose behavior warranted a police callout, or even an arrest."

The short, mustached sergeant nodded.

"You'll need to go through to the back office. The records are all kept there. But I'm not sure what you will be able to find, as Detective Sheldon has been following up on all the reports in the likelihood that the killer caused trouble earlier."

Leblanc felt disappointed that this theory had already been explored. Still, it had been worth a try, and perhaps it would also be a good idea to re-look at these reports. Sometimes, a fresh pair of eyes could spot new details, he knew.

"Go through, sir," the sergeant said, indicating the door to the right.

Leblanc headed to the door and opened it.

But, as soon as he walked into the corridor, he heard a buzz from the back office, and a moment later, Sheldon rushed out with car keys in his hand.

"Detective Leblanc," he said. "I was about to call you. We just got a report sent in by someone on site. They said they saw a stranger scoping out the construction area, and we're heading there right now to check it out. Are you able to come along?"

"Yes, of course," Leblanc agreed, feeling glad that he'd arrived at this time, as he and Katie were sharing a car, which she had taken. This way, he could ride with the police and join them in their search while Katie was speaking to the journalist.

He followed the officer to his car at a half-run.

There were two other police already waiting in the car.

Leblanc climbed in the back, shaking hands with the two quickly as Sheldon headed out.

"The report was of an aggressive-looking man, hiding in a tree and scoping the site out," Sheldon said, sounding excited, glancing back as he drove. "Two of the men in the eastern section of the site called it in. There's very little work being done on site today, which is probably why they're noticing any passers-by. We're looking for a tall, rangy individual with a short beard, wearing a camouflage jacket."

"It's good that they have such a clear description," Leblanc said.

Sheldon nodded. "People on site are nervous. Nobody wants any more deaths. We've had two false alarms today already. I nearly called you for one, but decided to check it out first. But this sounds genuine."

"How long has the person been there?"

"They think about ten minutes."

Sheldon sped down the bumpy track to the construction site. He stopped the car at the end of the road and they got out.

"If we head east from here, we'll come to the place he was spotted. They described it to me accurately. He was up a tall tree, about twenty yards from that outbuilding there, the one with the white roof."

"He was up a tree?"

"Yes. According to the eyewitnesses."

"I wonder if he's still there. If we come from this direction, we might surprise him," Leblanc observed.

"Yes, that's what I am hoping we can do," Sheldon agreed. "We'll go on foot from here, and fan out. Let's see if we can spot him. He may still be in place, but he might have picked up that he was seen, and be fleeing the area, or have moved to another vantage point. So we must stay alert."

They started walking, with Sheldon leading the way. Once they were past the white-roofed outbuilding, they fanned out, covering the wider area of woods beyond, moving slowly forward.

Leblanc felt glad to be part of this search as he paced forward, looking up and down, scanning the trees carefully, feeling tense and expectant that somewhere, the killer might be hiding and watching.

They were close to him now, if that was so. They couldn't let him get away. That time limit, to find him by sundown, tugged a knot of worry tight in his mind every time he thought of it.

He could hear footsteps and rustling faintly to either side of him as the others fanned out. He had his gun drawn and ready.

Sheldon was several yards away to his right. The detective was moving forward slowly, looking up ahead, and then behind, scanning the trees.

Leblanc moved slowly, sticking to the shadows. He was careful not to let twigs snap under his feet, or to disturb the leaves as he made his way through the woods.

His heart was beating fast. He was excited by the possibility of this being the person he was looking for. Let this be the killer and let us catch him, he pleaded to himself.

He came to the edge of a large tree and paused, scanning the tree line before him. The sun was lower in the sky now, and it cast his shadow onto the ground.

He couldn't see anyone up ahead.

Leblanc's eyes were locked on the trees. Where could this man be hiding? He wasn't in any of the branches, although Leblanc had checked carefully, knowing how a camouflage jacket might blend in with the green and brown of the foliage.

At the edge of his vision, Leblanc saw Sheldon pause to look around. He waved to Leblanc, indicating that he would be moving on to the left.

Leblanc nodded, and moved forward, still scanning the trees, looking for any sign of movement.

But as he walked, as he searched, he started to feel disappointed. It seemed less and less likely that this man was still around. They had checked every tree carefully. There had been no sign at all of him so far.

Leblanc couldn't let his attention waver, though. He narrowed his eyes, pacing forward, trying to maintain both his focus and his hope.

He turned his eyes downward, looking at the ground, hoping he might see a footprint, noting the broken twigs among the thick mat of leaves. Nothing that stood out, but the killer's tracks might be easy to miss, if he was trying to hide them. And the broken twigs did indicate someone had passed this way.

And then, ahead of him, he saw a flutter of movement.

He picked up the faint glimpse of a camouflage pattern in the trees. A rangy man was heading away from the construction site, moving fast and silently through the trees.

"There he is!" Leblanc felt excitement surge inside him. "He's there!"

He broke into a run.

But the man ahead of him looked around, and an expression of wary surprise settled on his face. He turned away from Leblanc and began running too, at a pace so fast that he seemed almost to melt away into the trees.

As the killer ran, Leblanc could see his camouflage jacket flapping on his back. He was running fast.

"Stop him!" Leblanc felt his heart pound as he gave chase. He heard cries from the rest of the party, who had seen what was happening and who were also closing in. But they were further away. He'd been on Leblanc's line, and Leblanc had the best chance of catching him.

He was not going to let this suspect get away. He was not! No matter what it took, he was going to find him and chase him down.

His feet thudded over the leaves as he sprinted into the trees, desperately trying to keep the fleeing man within his sights.

CHAPTER TWENTY FOUR

Katie jogged down the trail, feeling anxious and on edge as she headed into the forest. She didn't like anything about this setup. She was extremely uneasy about the fact that Brian Banner had gone out with a lone, female tourist who he'd said was planning to hike further, alone. That raised so many red flags. Brian must know what was happening in this area. Why would he have said such a thing unless he was trying to account for her having been alone when she died?

Surely no tour guide worth his salt would allow a woman into the woods solo, at a time when murders were occurring in the direct area?

Unless he was the killer himself?

All the signs were there. The aggression, the lack of reason, the threats and blame directed at harmless people.

Breathing hard but unwilling to slow down, Katie sprinted on.

The forest closed in around her as she ran, dark and oppressive. She could hear leaves rustling around her. She could see the patches of green moss on the tree trunks. And she could hear birds, a chorus of them from overhead, their sounds sharp and sweet in the otherwise quiet woods.

What she couldn't see were any paths leading off the trail. There was only one route to follow so far. There hadn't been any sign of anyone digressing from it into the thick undergrowth.

She raced down the trail, knowing she was moving in the right direction.

Reaching a place where the trees cleared, she glanced up at the sky. The sun was lower in the sky, and it cast deep shadows among the trees.

It was afternoon. The time limit that Scott had told them about was fast approaching.

And then, she dropped to a walk, treading quietly, because she saw she was approaching a natural clearing in the forest.

She glanced down, noting faint footsteps among the leaves and loose soil.

Ahead of her, to the right, she saw a small, wooden structure. It looked like it could be a birding hide. It was situated at the top of a slope. Beyond, the ground fell away and she could hear the trickling of a stream.

There was someone in the hide. She could see the silhouette faintly, and heard a heavy footstep.

Only one person. Her stomach clenched as she thought what that might mean.

Tense and alert, Katie moved forward, feeling the sensation of danger now, like a line of pins and needles tightening her skin.

The person was hidden from her view by the wooden walls of the hide. He - or she - wasn't moving now. Katie approached the hide carefully. It was a long, narrow structure.

"Brian Banner?" she called out.

She heard a sharp cry of alarm.

The next moment, an elderly man peered around the hide.

"You startled me," he said. "What do you want?"

"I'm looking for Brian Banner, the birder. I believe he came down this way," Katie said.

"I don't know about any birder. But a man walked this way a few minutes ago. Tall, with a brown hat on his head."

"Alone?" Katie asked.

"Alone," he replied.

She was starting to fear the worst. He should not have been alone.

She followed the side path that the elderly man had indicated, walking swiftly, picking her way through the logs and brush, past the low, sweeping branches. And then, she saw him ahead of her. A tall, rangy man wearing a brown hat.

He was looking up at a tree. As she watched, he reached out a hand, testing one of the branches. He looked about to swing himself up there. And he was alone. There was no sign of his client.

But with his hand raised, Katie clearly saw the firearm holstered at his hip. She was taking no chances. She drew her own gun.

"Brian Banner!" she called sharply.

He whirled around.

He stared at her in shock. He cried out. And then, he began to run.

"Stop!" Katie called out, following him, gun in hand.

He was powering away from the trail, heading into the denser part of the forest.

He ran with a smooth, powerful stride. She chased after him, her feet thudding on the earth as she raced along the tangled path.

He headed up the slope, towards the top of the natural clearing. The higher ground.

"Stop!" she cried out, her voice sharp and loud in the still, quiet forest.

He reached the top of the slope. He glanced back over his shoulder. She could see his face, his eyes, the hard set of his mouth. His expression was grim, and he looked tough and determined.

Then he ran on, sprinting across the clearing, heading for the denser part of the forest. She could hear her own breath in her ears, her quick footsteps on the leaf-strewn ground. And above that, ahead of her, she could hear his breathing, as hard and as fast as hers.

He reached the edge of the forest, disappearing into the thicker undergrowth. But he was faltering now. He had started out fast, but he wasn't a runner. He was flagging. She was going to get him. Katie powered into the trees.

And there he was. Leaning against a tree. Holding his side, as if he had a painful stitch. He turned to her with a terrified expression.

"Don't - don't shoot," he gasped.

She stared at him in surprise.

"Why were you running?" She was almost too breathless to get out the words.

"Why? Because you were running after me. I know what's going on here, man. I know they're targeting innocent people."

Close up, she saw that Brian was in his fifties, with sharp blue eyes, and a lean, solemn face.

Katie planted her feet firmly in the soil, and kept a hold on her gun.

"What do you mean?"

"I mean these evil people who are doing the construction work. I know for a fact that they're letting the criminal elements in. Innocent people are being killed. There are murderers roaming the forest now. I knew this would happen. I thought you were one of them. Are you one?"

He looked at her suspiciously, and seemed ready to run again.

"I'm FBI," Katie said.

"That doesn't necessarily let you off the hook." He frowned. "That's exactly the cover that these criminals might be using."

Katie was beginning to see why Simone from the North Minnesota News had experienced problems with this man. He definitely did not have a firm grasp on reality. But for now, her main concern was whether the woman with him was safe.

"I am FBI. And you ran from police. Therefore, I need to question you. I will use my firearm if you run again. This is a serious warning," she said, her voice sharp.

His eyes flickered from the gun to her face and back again.

Katie continued. "Your office said you took a woman out here, and that you were going to let her hike on her own," Katie said. "Where is she? That's my first question."

"She's in the south hide. Up the hill." He turned and pointed. "I was walking this way to the north hide."

"And you were leaving her on her own? After all these killings have occurred?"

"She's a photographer. She wanted to be left alone there for hours. But I wanted to keep her safe, so I thought the best solution was to go to the opposite hide, where I'd be out of her way, and still have a good view of her."

Katie wasn't sure if she believed this, but it would be easy to prove.

She stepped back, scanning the hide on the other side of the small valley.

Sure enough, through the boards, she could see movement, and the flash of a blue jacket. A moment later, she glimpsed a woman with a long camera lens, pointing it upward at a treetop.

So the photography story was correct. But what about his alibi?

"You have been threatening the local media. Complaining about the development. So I need to account for your whereabouts last night, and early this morning," she said.

"Early this morning, I took a group of three tourists on our sunrise birding tour," he explained. "With these tours, we leave at four a.m. and are in the woods by the time it gets light. We got back at eight this morning. I had breakfast, and then headed out with Mary-Ann here."

"Can you confirm this earlier booking?"

"Yes. My office can confirm it. They'll have all the details. The tourists were from Ohio. Very keen birders. They were like-minded souls. We spotted a chemtrail as well as an American Golden Plover, and had a good chat about the people who are controlling things, up there." He gestured vaguely skyward.

Finally, Katie lowered her gun. She didn't think that Brian was well-grounded in reality at all, and he had all the hallmarks of a conspiracy theorist. But if the office checked out his alibi, then she didn't think he was guilty of the murders. Because at four a.m. he'd been ready to take out a group of birders. He hadn't been seeking victims in the woods near the site.

"Thank you," she said.

As she turned away, walking through the quiet woods and listening to the chorus of birdsong, she began thinking hard.

This had been the wrong lead. But she didn't think it had necessarily been the wrong direction. She thought it was a very valid direction. People who believed their environment was being threatened would backlash severely against the development going ahead. The kills, on and near the site, had effectively created an atmosphere of fear and had halted operations. That had been their main effect.

And she'd missed a nuance earlier on.

Simone had said to her that Brian was the only person in town who had complained so vociferously about the development. But Ashton was a small town and there were other towns nearby.

She was going to give the journalist a call, she decided, and ask what complaints the media had received from the nearby towns or the wider area.

Katie was convinced that if she followed this line of thought, there would be more.

She picked up the phone and dialed Simone's number while walking back to her car.

"Can I help?" Simone asked. Katie could hear the clinking of cups and the hiss of the coffee machine in the background.

"Simone, when I was speaking to you earlier, you mentioned Brian Banner had been the only complainant in town who threatened you. Were there others, outside of this town, who also tried to create trouble at the site?"

Simone responded instantly.

"Yes. It wasn't an individual, though, but rather an environmental action group. It's called Greentrees, and it's based in Crewe, about fifty miles from here. They staged several protests on site, which we covered. One of them did get violent, if I recall. But they've been quiet for a few weeks now and haven't been in contact with us for a while."

Katie thought that could be significant. Had the group, or its leader, or even a rogue member, come up with another means of sabotaging the development? Without a doubt, this needed to be her next step.

"Please give me the details of this group," she said.

CHAPTER TWENTY FIVE

Leblanc powered after the fleeing man, keeping his flapping camouflage jacket in view. As he passed by a splash of sunshine in the clearing, he saw his shadow, long and dark, racing alongside him. It reminded him that the minutes until sunset were shortening, and they had an impossible deadline to meet.

This man was a fast sprinter, but Leblanc was faster. He was fit. He'd worked on his sprinting daily, down the streets of Sault Ste. Marie, and also along the rocky and uneven trails outside of the town.

He knew he was fit and he knew he was fast. He ran with a long, powerful stride. The man ahead was getting tired. He was starting to stumble and falter. He was still fast, but he was not as fast.

Leblanc was closing in. He leaped over a log, landing easily on the other side.

He saw the man glance back over his shoulder. He seemed to realize he was being outpaced. But it didn't stop him. Instead, he darted left, leaving the trail and crashing through the undergrowth.

It was thick here, but Leblanc was able to follow, pushing aside the branches, dodging the brambles. The ground was steeper and he had to watch his step. The trees were close together, and he could feel their branches brush his face.

Behind him he could hear the cries of the team following.

He was in the deeper woods now, and the trees were close together. It was cooler, shadier. The sunlight didn't reach here.

Leblanc rushed through the thorny undergrowth, ignoring the scratches on his arms. He was going to catch him. It felt like a personal mission, something he was doing for the task force, for Katie, for his own future.

He was closing in. The man ahead was stumbling again. His face was glistening with sweat.

He could get him now. With a cry, Leblanc charged forward. He was almost on top of his suspect, who was faltering and stumbling, hands on his knees. Leblanc reached for his shoulder, grasping for the back of his jacket.

He felt the material turn and pull in his hands. He pulled it to the side, ready to wrap his arms around the man's shoulders and bring him to the ground.

But before he could do that, the man cringed away, holding his hands high in the air.

"What - what's going on here? What are you doing? Look, I'm sorry! I'm sorry!"

Leblanc rested his hands on his thighs. The chase had taken everything out of him. Talking and breathing, for a moment, was impossible. Finally he puffed out the words.

"Sorry? For what?"

How far, exactly, did this apology go, he wondered for a confused moment.

He was facing a man who lived up to the description. He was tall, rangy, with a short beard. The camo jacket was faded and not new.

But the man's blue eyes were surprisingly direct and they were focused on Leblanc.

"Well, okay. I came into a restricted area, yes, I have been in the woods, I've been to the construction site. I know I'm guilty. I read the notices and shouldn't have gone further. I apologize. I just don't see why I'm being treated like a criminal."

"What?" Leblanc asked, feeling stunned by the words.

"I'm sorry for running away. I should have stayed put and accepted the punishment. What do I get? A fine? I mean, what is the penalty?"

Yet again, his words were surprising Leblanc, who had no idea what he meant.

"The penalty for what?"

"That notice a few hundred yards from the construction site said that trespassers were not allowed and that there would be penalties." He gazed in surprise at the gathering police. "I just didn't know they would be this strongly enforced. You guys really do have a no tolerance policy!"

"We're not pursuing you because you violated the boundaries." Leblanc glared at the breathless man. "Are you aware murders have been committed here?"

The man gaped at Leblanc, looking shocked. Then he shook his head. "I'm sorry, no. Not at all. I didn't know that. I've been driving back from Manitoba for the last two days. I was up north, visiting a friend. I decided to stop off and do some hunting in the woods before I went back home. But I saw the construction and the signs and I was curious."

Leblanc sighed inwardly. At first glance it seemed this was truly an innocent citizen who had just been in the wrong place at the wrong time. But he was taking nobody's word for what they said. Not when lives were at stake.

"I need to see some ID," he said.

The man blinked. Slowly, he reached into his pocket and produced a wallet.

"Here."

Leblanc rifled through the wallet, pulling out a driver's license, a fishing license, and some store loyalty cards. There was a photograph of the man next to his name.

"Michael Holmes. That is who you are?"

The man nodded, looking at the wallet in Leblanc's hand.

"Do you have proof of your trip?"

He nodded. "I've got my car parked nearby. It's down the road a ways. There's a parking pass in the window from the nature preserve where we hiked. I stayed in a motel last night, and left early for the final leg of the drive. So I can show you that booking, too. They had a camera in the lobby that would have recorded me checking in and out."

He handed the wallet back.

"I'll escort this gent to his car and get proof of the trip," one of the police offered.

"Thanks," Leblanc said. He turned to the hunter. "Please, leave the area now. It's not safe. Until we've caught the person who's committing the crimes, everyone is at risk."

The man nodded somberly. "I will. And I'm sorry for taking up your time."

Leblanc's shoulders sagged in defeat. He was not their suspect. He was a curious bystander, passing through, who had been in the wrong place at the wrong time.

He felt like he was chasing a ghost.

How was Katie doing? Perhaps she had better luck on her side?

He felt a flare of worry as he realized she hadn't checked in yet. What was happening; was she alright?

Quickly, he picked up his phone and dialed her number.

It rang and rang for long enough that he started getting the familiar sick twist of anxiety in his stomach.

Then she picked up.

"Leblanc," she said. "Any news?"

"We chased down a suspect. He was just a curious bystander passing through. So no, it didn't check out," he admitted. "What about you?"

"I think I might have something," she said. "My first lead didn't check out, but I called the local journalist again and I've got a new lead. This one, I think is more promising. In fact, we need to move on it right away."

"That sounds good," he said, feeling heartened after the disappointment of a few minutes ago.

"Where are you? I'll come past and pick you up and then I'll tell you where I think we need to go."

She sounded excited. Leblanc felt encouraged. He was suddenly certain, from the tone of her voice, that this next lead would take them where they needed to be.

CHAPTER TWENTY SIX

"We were on the right track when we were looking for people who had issues with the development," Katie told Leblanc as soon as he climbed into the car. She stared at him excitedly. "We just didn't widen the parameters enough."

"So, what is it?" he asked.

"Simone sent me all the information. Look here," she said. She opened her phone and showed him a photo of a pamphlet.

On the front of it was a chopped down tree with a red line through it, and a skull and crossbones.

"Stop the Destruction," the heading read.

"These were circulated all over town a month ago, when the site clearing first began. The organization has been keeping the pressure on since then - but apparently in the last couple of weeks they have been much quieter."

"The organization being?"

"It's an environmental organization known as Greentrees. They are very active in the county, and they oppose everything that they feel will damage the environment. From mining to deforestation, to factories that pollute the surroundings."

"And why didn't we pick up on this earlier?" Leblanc asked, as Katie programmed the GPS taking them fifty miles south. It was going to be an hour's drive and she found herself automatically glancing at the clock and the sky.

Time was ticking by. If they were wrong, this was going to be an extremely expensive hour. It could cost them everything. But they were not going to be wrong. They were going to be right. She was sure of it.

"We didn't pick up on it earlier because they're not local, and because they are based in Crewe, a couple of towns over, and because they have been less active recently. But they have opposed the development ever since it started. Especially at first," she said.

"What did they do?" Leblanc asked.

"They approached the media. They protested on site. I saw reports that they were hands-on in that regard. They tried to stop the process physically. A couple of the members were detained after harassing and assaulting workers. But it was early on in the project, and neither of the members was from this town, which is why we didn't pick it up here. They even went after the developers of the project via the local district attorney's office."

"And?" he asked.

"Nothing happened," she said. "The case against them was dismissed."

"They clearly have funding and leverage, though?" Leblanc observed.

"Yes, they do. They raise money, based on membership dues and grants, and they fund through donation drives," she said. "But Simone mentioned that in the past, they have gotten into trouble. Members get passionate about causes and end up threatening, or damaging property, or getting involved in defamation lawsuits."

"So, they are a well-funded opposition group that tends to go too far," Leblanc said.

"They are, so someone from the group may have been involved in the crimes that have occurred at the development site," Katie said. "The founder's name is Robin Moxley, and he's got a history of doing this himself. He and three other members were arrested a few years ago for harassment of developers. That was also settled out of court."

"So are they based in Crewe?"

"Yes. It's where their headquarters are, and most of their membership comes from there, too. It's a much bigger town. And they do have a permanent headquarters, by the side of an agricultural store."

Katie gripped the wheel. She needed to cover this distance as fast as they could. This organization was an unknown entity but they needed to uncover its identity, and learn which of its members might have taken a murderous step in their efforts to protect this local forest.

*

Fifty minutes later, Katie pulled up outside the agricultural store, set in a rural area outside Crewe, which was about five times the size of Ashton, and definitely a busier place.

The organization had set the headquarters up in a large wooden cabin, which Katie guessed had either been donated by a member, or built through funding. The sign outside advertised them. Greentrees Environmental Group.

"Here we are," Katie said. "Let's go in."

The agricultural store next door was busy with feed trucks and cars coming and going, driving in and out of the large parking lot. But Greentrees seemed to have a few cars parked near this section of the paving, and Katie hoped that some of the members would be here.

She got out and walked up the path to the front door. Through the windows, she noticed that the walls inside were papered with posters.

"Stop the Oil Drilling"

"Say No to the Pipeline"

"Stop the Deforestation"

There was the same picture she'd seen on the pamphlet, of the chopped down tree with the red line through it. Feeling determined, Katie tapped on the door, which was ajar, before pushing it open and stepping in.

Inside, there were three people at work, sitting at desks near the wooden walls.

The closest one, a brown haired woman with a tattoo of a flower on her arm, looked up.

"Can I help you?" she asked.

"We're looking for Robin Moxley," Katie said.

The woman's gaze immediately went to the door at the back of the room.

"He's in a meeting with the committee members." She said it in a way that indicated this meeting would not be interrupted.

"We're police," Katie said briefly. "It's police business, and urgent."

The woman sprang to her feet, looking alarmed.

"If you don't mind, I'll just go through and check with them," she said, hurrying across the wooden floor. She opened the adjoining door, and Katie heard the brief buzz of voices before it closed behind her.

A moment later, it opened again and she came out.

"Please, go through," she invited them.

Katie stepped into a smaller room dominated by a round wooden table. Five people were sitting at it, three men and two women. The man at the far side of the table stood up immediately.

He was a spry, gray-haired man with a short goatee and bright blue eyes.

"I'm Robin Moxley, founder and chairman of Greentrees," he said. "And you are?"

"Agent Winter and Detective Leblanc," Katie said. "We're investigating the murders that have been taking place on the construction site near Ashton."

117

"Ah, yes." Moxley met their gaze unblinkingly. "That's a terrible thing. Greentrees is not responsible for that. Not in any way. Let me show you the reports, and our police clearance."

He stood up and hurried around the table.

Friendly as he was, Katie noticed the other committee members were clearly less so. The two redheaded women, who looked like they might be sisters, were glowering at her. The man closest to them, suave and gray-haired, was also looking angrily in their direction.

And the blonde man on the far side, who was a tall, lean, and fit=looking man in his thirties, wasn't meeting their eyes at all. He was looking down at the desk.

Katie's sharp eyes picked up a recent graze on the back of the blonde man's hand and wrist that looked to be deep, and was freshly scabbed over. She wondered how he'd gotten that graze.

"Come through, come through," Moxley invited them, interrupting her thoughts.

She and Leblanc turned and retraced their steps to the front office where he headed purposefully to a filing cabinet.

"Our organization does not condone violence. It's true that two of our members did get into a confrontation with police during our public demonstrations outside the Ashton site, but there was fault on both sides and the charges were dropped. Here's the folder which contains all the details."

He handed it to Katie, who stood at the desk, looking through it. Leblanc stood alongside, reading with the same speed and intensity.

Katie was sure Leblanc was also concluding that this didn't seem to be nearly as simple as Moxley was discounting it to be. This had been a complex case, and the police had done a thorough job in presenting the charges.

Two Greentrees members had attacked site workers, resulting in minor injuries to one worker, but the site workers had drawn firearms and threatened them in turn. A shot had in fact been fired by one of the workers, which had meant that both sides had been blamed for escalating the situation, Katie read.

"Were any of the committee members involved?" she asked, thinking again about that graze on the blond man's arm.

"Yes, one of them," Moxley said. He spoke reluctantly as if he was not keen to give this information.

"Which one?"

118

"Brady Cole. He's inside the meeting room. He's one of our most fiery young activists. He takes cases on with passion. Yes, in this case, he overstepped the mark, but it's no reflection on his character. It was simply that he was trying to physically restrain one of the workers from entering the site."

Katie felt another flicker of interest. Brady Cole must be the younger man inside, the one who hadn't met their eyes, the one with the graze.

"He is injured, I noticed. His right wrist is grazed," Leblanc said, and Katie felt a flare of excitement he was on the same page.

"Yes. That was nothing to do with the confrontation, which was weeks ago. He does climbing. He injured himself while out on the rock face, I believe." Moxley gave them a suave smile.

Climbing?

The pieces were falling into place for Katie.

"I'd like to speak to Brady Cole, if you don't mind," she said.

Moxley looked surprised. "You would? Sure, I guess you can."

He pushed open the door to the meeting room and Katie walked through.

But with a twist of her stomach, she saw the chair where Brady had been sitting was now empty.

"Where did he go?" Moxley asked the others, sounding surprised.

The closest redheaded woman answered.

"He didn't say. He just got up and went out of the back door there, as soon as you had left the room," she said.

Katie looked at Leblanc.

Their suspect was fleeing. She was sure of it.

He'd known he was in trouble from the time they'd arrived, and now he was looking to get away before it landed on him.

CHAPTER TWENTY SEVEN

"What car does Brady Cole drive?" Katie asked the environmental committee members, her voice urgent. They would need to get an APB out if he'd fled in a vehicle.

"He drives a black Jeep," the redheaded woman said, sounding anxious, her voice unsteady. "But - but he didn't bring it here today. He came with us. We gave him a ride."

"Is there any reason for him to have left the meeting room?"

"No, none. I mean, we'd started our meeting half an hour ago. He was about to present a report. That back door doesn't lead anywhere except the agricultural store's backyard. The restroom is accessed via the front room," the woman stammered.

So Brady was fleeing for sure, and he was doing it on foot. That changed the landscape of what they needed to do, and where they must look.

"If he comes back in here, do not let him go. We need to question him. That is a direct order," Katie said.

Then there was no more time to waste. She rushed across the conference room and pushed open the back door, taking the same route Brady had done as he'd fled out of the building and into the yard where the agricultural supplies store was located.

"I'll check the road," Leblanc shouted, veering to the right.

"I'll search the yard," she called back.

There were only two of them, and it was a big area, but hopefully they could cover the only two directions it would have been possible for this man to take.

He'd been wearing a green shirt, Katie remembered, as she rushed down the paved drive.

She raced into the agricultural store yard. It was a busy place.

There were three large trucks parked near the building, and two men were unloading a pallet of fertilizer from one of them. They looked up in surprise as Katie rushed past them. She saw a small van pull in, and a man in a checkered shirt hurry towards it, holding two large bags.

Would he have gone into the building itself? She hesitated. If she was him, she wouldn't have done that, but would have fled into the large outside storage area, where pallets piled high with bags and bales offered a checkerboard of hiding places.

She rushed down into the yard, ignoring the inquiring shout from one of the workers, keeping a lookout for the tall, rangy man in the green shirt. Green shirt. Was that him? She veered briefly left but saw she was wrong. It was a woman in a green jacket.

Katie's heart was pounding. They could not afford to lose this suspect. Not when the afternoon shadows were lengthening and he had a clear history of sabotaging the site. If he got away, the consequences would be unthinkable. They had to find him and catch him.

Katie darted alongside the wall of the building. She raced over the hard-packed earth of the yard, the heels of her shoes digging in. He had to hide, or run. Those were his only options. She guessed he was hiding and looking to run.

She heard a loud clang from the direction of the store, and whirled around. But it was just one of the pallets being loaded onto a truck.

She turned right and ran along the rows of bags and bales, searching for a man in a green shirt, looking for any sign of him hiding, or running, or waiting in cover.

Katie ran to the edge of the building, looking right and left. The only other people here were a couple loading up a small truck, who looked at her in surprise.

Where on earth had he gone? Despair clenched at her stomach. He couldn't have gotten away. Not now, not at this critical time.

She saw nothing. She came to the end of the rows and stopped. He was nowhere in sight.

At the far end, a man in a checkered shirt was walking back to the van, holding two bags. There was a woman in riding breeches waiting for bags to be loaded, and a farm worker in a gray overall.

No green shirt.

She spun around again. And then, she saw him.

He was walking swiftly between two of the tall pallets of bags, heading for the wire gate at the bottom of the site, where delivery trucks were being routed to offload their contents.

"He's there!" Katie shouted as loud as she could. She knew she would alert him by shouting, but she hoped that Leblanc would also hear her because she knew it might take the two of them to chase him down.

121

And then, there was no more time for shouting.

Katie began to run, knowing she would need all of her power and speed to catch up with this strong, athletic man.

And he'd seen her. His head whipped around. His body tensed. Without a doubt, he was alerted to her presence and looking to escape.

She saw his eyes widen.

"Brady Cole," she shouted. "We need to speak to you."

But he turned in the direction of the dirt track and began sprinting away from her.

"Brady Cole!" she shouted again, but he was already several yards away, heading for the open gate. He was in full flight.

Katie started to run, pounding over the uneven ground and dodging between the piles of bags and bales. The wind was flapping the tarpaulins and the shadows were lengthening, creating pools of darkness as she ran. Behind her, she heard yells and cries of alarm as people saw the chase.

Brady was going out. He darted toward the gate, with Katie close behind. She ran at full speed, kicking up dust and gravel, following the aggressive stride of the man who was her prime suspect.

He'd gotten to the gate. He was heading through it and pounding down the sand road beyond.

She could not let him get away, but nor could she catch him. He was too fast for her and fear clenched at her again, lending her a new surge of speed. This was not a moment for saying no. This was a moment for giving it everything she had, in the knowledge that her entire future hinged on this capture.

And then, ahead of her, she saw Leblanc, and her heart leaped.

He'd heard her shout and he'd seen what was playing out. Leblanc had run down from the main road, around the edge of the building, and was now heading toward Brady at a full run.

Brady skidded to a stop. Katie could see his chest heaving in panic, his gaze veering from side to side as he considered his options.

Clearly deciding on Katie as the weaker target, he turned toward her and began sprinting down the road, on the opposite side. He must be hoping that he'd be able to force his way past her if she got to him in time, using his weight and speed to blast through her defenses.

She saw that in a moment. But he had underestimated her.

Katie flew toward him with all the remaining strength in her legs. She launched herself at him in a flying tackle. She grabbed him around the waist.

Her speed and weight were enough. Brady was flung off balance. He crashed to the ground, with Katie still clinging on.

Yelling and shouting, Brady turned to her, fists flying, his legs kicking out at her. Katie took a punch to the neck. His fist slammed into her and her head snapped back, but she wasn't letting go.

She managed to keep hold of him, her right hand still reaching for his wrist, her fingers digging in. She hooked her arm around his neck, but his legs were flailing, the heavy boots kicking out at her.

And then, Leblanc arrived.

He launched himself at the man, grabbing his right arm, dragging him away from Katie so that he skidded along the dirt track.

Immediately, Katie was on her feet, grabbing onto Brady's left arm as he cursed and threatened in breathless tones. But they had him. He was handcuffed.

The fast, reckless and aggressive suspect had not managed to make his getaway.

It was two hours to sundown, Katie estimated. They had just two hours to confirm his guilt, and make the arrest.

CHAPTER TWENTY EIGHT

Katie walked into the interview room at the Crewe police department. This town was large enough to have a full police headquarters, and here, Brady could be detained.

She felt tension thrumming inside her.

Moxley and the two redheaded committee members were waiting in the lobby of the police department. Moxley was already on the phone, and Katie was sure he was getting legal advice. She could see they were extremely worried by what had just happened. She wondered if they knew more than they were telling.

They had a lot of evidence against Brady. He'd been on site, he'd threatened workers. He had a fresh graze on his hand, exactly the sort of injury a person might get when hauling a body high up a tree. But they needed his testimonial. Katie could not afford any gray areas in this case. Not with so much at stake. They needed this wrapped up as tight as it could go.

Brady Cole had clearly been guilty enough to run from them, and to disappear from the environmental group meeting as soon as he had realized that the police were asking questions. That represented a strong starting point.

She stepped into the room, with Leblanc behind her.

Brady was seated on the far side of the desk, facing the door. His head was bowed, his eyes trained on the table in front of him. His short blonde hair looked ruffled. The graze had split open in the scuffle and was oozing blood again.

"Mr. Cole," she said. "We're investigating the recent murders on the construction site. We know that you are on the committee of the group who opposed this deforestation, and that you were arrested on site for physically interfering with workers."

He lifted his head and stared at her defiantly. His eyes were like chips of ice. She did not see the faintest trace of readiness to confess.

"The group's legal team handled that incident," he said in a deep voice. "Charges were dropped."

"Even so, it indicates to me that you felt strongly enough to intervene personally, and to go above and beyond the law in trying to stop this construction," Katie emphasized.

Brady shrugged. "Fault on both sides. They pulled guns on us. Read the report," he muttered.

"What were your movements last night?" she pressured him. "Can you account for your time last night? And in the early hours of this morning?"

He stared at her again. The silence stretched out, intense and uncomfortable.

"Last night I was at home," he said.

"Your residence is here, in Crewe?"

"On the outskirts of town, yes."

"Can anyone confirm your whereabouts at home?"

He shook his head. "I live alone."

"And the night before that?" Katie pressured.

Brady drew in a deep breath. He shook his head slowly.

"I am not going to answer your questions. I demand my lawyer."

"Your whereabouts the night before?" Katie tried one more time. "You need to tell us, Mr. Cole."

He stared at her, his cold eyes holding hers.

"I'm not going to tell you anything," he said.

"Are you refusing to answer these questions?" she asked.

She was steeling herself for an outburst. She had a feeling he might explode, but at the last moment, he controlled himself, drawing in a deep breath.

"I'm not saying more until my lawyer gets here," he said.

"Why not?" Katie pushed him, hoping to get him back to that moment where he'd been about to snap. "Where were you between the hours of three and five a.m. this morning? Why do you have a problem telling us this?"

He turned his gaze back to the table. His expression had hardened.

"I am not going to disclose any more information without my lawyer present," he said firmly. "It's my right. I have a right to have legal representation."

"Then you need to make a call," she said. "We won't be releasing you until we have all of our questions answered."

There was a phone on the wall of the interview room. Katie checked the line was open, and then passed it to Brady.

"I need to look up his number," he complained.

Katie took his own phone out of the secure box where it was stored. She didn't want him deleting anything else on the phone. She watched carefully as he looked up a number in his contacts, and dialed. Then she took his own phone away again.

"Can I speak to Bisset, please," he said. "Yes, it's urgent. I'm in police custody. I need him to come here and represent me."

He waited, listened.

"Okay, what time?"

Katie felt her stomach clench again.

"Fine, but please, tell him to hurry. I'm here at the police department in Crewe."

He disconnected. "My lawyer will be here in two hours."

That took them past sundown, Katie acknowledged, with a thud of her heart. Due to nothing more than logistical delays, they would not be able to interrogate this suspect fully until the deadline had passed.

He was giving all the signs of being guilty. But until they had completed the full interrogation, Katie could not be sure, and that was worrying her deeply.

"You must stay here until he arrives," she said firmly.

She stepped out of the room and closed the door.

"Okay," Leblanc said. He stared at her, looking as fraught as she felt. "There's a lot we can do in the meantime. We can interview the other committee members – after all, they are here and waiting. We can go to Brady's home, search his house, look for any evidence, any plans. Speak to the neighbors. Perhaps there are cameras along the route somewhere and we can pick up his vehicle."

"I think all those will be helpful. But what if it isn't him? Remember, this is his style, Leblanc. When I was reading the report, it stuck in my mind that he did exactly the same thing last time he was charged. He refused to speak, got his lawyer involved, and the charges were dropped. I am sure he's going to do the same again. He's just being cautious. He's one of those guys."

Leblanc let out a frustrated sigh.

"If only we did not have this damned deadline looming over us. We can't do half a job, Katie."

"We can't, but we also can't give up what we have. We have a strong suspect in custody. There's a likelihood he is our guy."

But they needed more, and there wasn't time.

At that moment, Katie's phone rang.

It was Scott on the line, and she felt her heart flip-flop, because he, too, was going to need to make the call to the powers that would decide the task force's future, or its fate.

She walked down the corridor in the opposite direction from the lobby and took the call.

"Any news, Katie?" Scott asked.

"We have a strong suspect in custody," she said. "He's part of an environmental group that opposed the development and in fact, he was arrested for interference and assault a couple of weeks ago. The charges were dropped. But he's not talking now, and he is insisting on lawyering up. His lawyer will be here in a couple of hours, which means it will be well after sundown by the time we've concluded the interviews."

Scott let out a frustrated sigh. "What do I tell them? Will this suspect hold up?"

"The evidence is pointing that way," Katie said. "But my problem with him is that he's done this before. He lawyers up and then he gets the charges dropped. It may well be he's just the kind of person who wants legal counsel with him before stating any facts."

"Do we have any other suspect whatsoever?"

"We don't. So we're going to check him out as much as we can before the lawyer arrives. We're going to search his house, see if we can track his car, look for evidence."

Katie tried not to think about the flimsy likelihood of finding real camera evidence in this sparsely populated area, with back roads aplenty, in a fifty mile distance between two small towns.

"Do I tell them we have a suspect?" Scott pressured her.

Biting her lip, Katie made the decision.

"Yes. Say we are busy with the final interrogation," she said. "We'll provide more information as soon as we have concluded our report in a couple of hours."

"I'll tell them that," Scott said, and she could hear the warning tone in his voice before he disconnected. He knew that what she said was a semi-bluff; it was buying them just a little more time. But it now meant that serious trouble potentially lay ahead.

Because Katie was not convinced.

She was fairly sure, but not totally sure. She did not believe beyond all doubt, that they had the killer in custody. Circumstances were pointing toward it, but there was still room for error.

If Brady was not the suspect, Katie knew she had better find someone who was, within the timeframe. Because after sundown, the governor was going to be baying for proof. And if Katie could not provide that proof, she would have sunk the unit, and it would be disbanded in disgrace.

"I'm going to start with the investigation into Brady's home, and his movements," Leblanc said worriedly. "I'll take the car and go there now."

"I'll go and speak to the other members of the conservation group," Katie said.

They were waiting in the lobby and were clearly there to plead for Brady Cole to be released. But perhaps, one of them might provide evidence that finally provided the missing piece in what they had.

It was Katie's only remaining hope, as she headed to the lobby. Perhaps one of the committee might be able to cast the final shaft of light into the gray areas that still lurked, disturbingly, within this case.

CHAPTER TWENTY NINE

As soon as Katie walked into the lobby, Moxley stepped forward.

"Agent, I know that this looks bad. It's not a good situation. But I want to plead with you not to let our organization's name get dragged into this, and also to put in a good word for Brady's character."

"You want to do that?" Katie asked. "Explain why?"

"I would just like to say that we, as a group, decided to back off from our criticism of the proposed development a while ago. I have known Brady for years and I don't believe he would be a person to commit such crimes. Most definitely, he was not doing so because we were still opposed to the deforestation."

"Why did he run, then?" Katie asked reflexively.

"Look, I don't know." Moxley spread his arms, looking anxious. "I don't know why he ran. I know he was expecting that there might be further consequences after his run-in with the site workers. That one of them might sue him for personal injury. He felt very guilty about that. And yes, he did interfere with them. His actions were out of line. I can't argue with that. All I can say is that our members are extremely passionate about protecting the fragile environment and it sometimes does have unintended consequences."

Now his words were sinking in, Katie felt interested by something else he'd said.

"Why did you back off from your criticism of the development? What changed?"

"Oh, we actually managed to have an effect through our intervention." Moxley took a deep breath and glanced at the women standing with him. Now, he looked more confident. "In fact, we backed off because they did make some changes and agreed to our proposed conditions, which made us more comfortable with the proposed development. You see, we're not opposed to all development. Just opposed to irresponsible development that threatens the environment unduly. That's what people don't understand about us."

"I see," Katie said. But there was no stopping Moxley, who anxiously wanted to elaborate on exactly what they had achieved.

"You see, we had some very valid concerns about that site. For a start, we were worried about some of the biggest trees, and the area going to the west of the site, which contains vulnerable species and some endangered trees. They then agreed to make changes to the layout to exclude those areas to preserve the trees, which they agreed were our heritage."

"Absolutely," one of the redheaded women agreed. "They were reasonable in the end. It took a lot of effort, but eventually they saw it our way."

"We also had issues with some of the construction materials used, which we reached agreement on also, and we insisted that no work would be done in the trees during nesting season, which is why they have been clearing the forest so fast, before the nests are built. And finally, we were very concerned about the risk of fire."

"Fire?" Katie asked.

"It's a huge risk on a site like that. And they had very few precautions in place. We had to keep pressuring the developers for better precautions and also for adequate off-site monitoring, which is not within their scope of responsibility. Just a week ago, we succeeded in getting the county forest management to bring in the local fire watch earlier than planned. I believe that individual is now monitoring the site, up in the trees, keeping an eye out for any fires that might be caused nearby by workers smoking, people coming and going, crew members lighting cooking fires – that sort of thing. That was the final condition that was met."

Katie's mind had latched onto this.

A fire watch? Nobody had mentioned this person was already on site. Carver had referred to the fire watch, and had said they would be taking up position in the future.

"Who is this fire watch?" she asked.

Moxley shook his head. "I don't know his name. He's one of a few hired by the county on a seasonal basis. He usually works from midsummer to early winter, through the dry season, until the rains start, you know, looking out for forest fires and the like at night. But they brought him in earlier this year, thanks to our pressure. And it took some pressure for them to bring the timeframe forward. I guess they didn't want to incur the costs of paying him, although they said the delay was because his mother recently died."

"She did?"

Katie felt very glad for Moxley's earnest outpourings, because they were starting to add up. And this was starting to paint a very relevant picture.

A man who'd recently had access to the site, and had free rein in the forest at night, unnoticed and unseen by the construction crew, employed directly by the county. And furthermore, a man who'd recently had a major life event take place.

The death of a mother could have precipitated a psychotic episode in a damaged or abused person. It could have set him on the path to being a killer.

She felt shocked that nobody had mentioned this man being on site until now, but she could see why there had been a lack of communication. The county forestry board was in a different governmental silo and the fire watch reported to the board, not the developers. They hadn't communicated directly with the developers about the fire watch's earlier arrival, but had only agreed to the conditions of the environmental group.

"I'm grateful you told me this," she said to Moxley. "We will take it into account. We can't do anything further until Brady's lawyer gets here. But for now, I need to rush back to site." She was about to turn away, but then she turned back to Moxley.

"The person you spoke to at the forestry board. Do you have their number?"

"Sure," Moxley said. "She's the secretary. Wendy Dewey. Here's her number."

She realized that Leblanc had taken the SUV and gone to search Brady's house. There wasn't time to wait for him. Not when every minute counted in checking out this new lead.

She hurried over to the officer in the lobby.

"Can I sign out a police vehicle?" she asked. "It's urgent."

"Sure," he said.

While Katie was waiting for the paperwork to be done, she quickly messaged Leblanc.

"I'm going after one last suspect. The fire watch. He overnights in trees near the site, watching for fire. He was brought in a week ago by the county forestry board. To me, it's adding up."

She sent the message and then grabbed the car keys, wondering how fast she would be able to get back to site, and if the suspicions she had about this man would be realized.

131

While Katie drove, she dialed Wendy Dewey's number, hoping that she would pick up, and she would be able to learn more as she accelerated along the quiet road.

Wendy answered on the fifth ring, just as Katie was preparing to leave an urgent voicemail.

"Good evening?" she said.

It was evening now. The sun was setting in a blaze of gold. Katie was acutely aware how short their remaining time was now.

"Ms. Dewey, it's FBI agent Winter here. I'm calling to ask you some questions in connection with an investigation."

"Sure. What do you want to know?" she said curiously.

"The fire watch that you deployed in the forest near Ashton. How long has he been on duty?"

"Since last Sunday," she replied. "It's very early in the season, but we did it to appease an environmental group that had concerns about a bigger fire risk in the area."

"And who is he? Do you know him well?"

"Fairly well, yes, as he's a local from my town. His name's Andrew Hunt. He's one of only a few seasonal workers we use. We've employed him for about six years now, and he's twenty-five years old. To be honest, it's not easy to find reliable fire watch workers. The job is very hard, the hours are long, and the pay is average," she confessed.

"What's his background?"

"He doesn't have a criminal record. We wouldn't hire anyone like that," she said quickly. Katie waited. After a pause, she spoke. "Look, I do know he was from a broken home, and his mother was an alcoholic. I know he got removed from her and put into temporary care a few times over the years, but even so, he looked after her. She passed away three weeks ago, and he then told us he was ready for duty last week. The environmental group was pressuring us to get someone there, so we used him. I hope there are no issues with him? He's a very quiet man. Obsessed with birds, which is why I guess the job suits him." She laughed.

Katie realized with a spark of excitement that this this checked another box, linking strongly to the bodies that had seemed to be arranged in nests.

"What area would he work in?" she asked.

"That's up to him. As long as he has a clear view of the forest through the night, the site he chooses is up to him," Wendy explained.

"Do you have a phone number for him?"

"I do, but not on me. It's at the office, and the department is all locked up for the night now. I can get it for you tomorrow morning, if you like? Of course, he does have his phone on him, and if there's a fire, he'll make all the relevant calls, and alert people in the area by means of a whistle and flare."

"If I need it, I'll let you know. Thank you," Katie said. She cut the call, concentrating on her driving, her mind buzzing with what she had just learned as she approached the site.

The fire watch would be on duty now. But how could she find him? Where, in all the trees, would he be hiding?

Carver met her at the entrance to the site, his face anxious. As she got out, Katie realized how quiet the site was, with all the workers off shift, and most of them off site. The silence felt expectant.

"Are there any leads, Agent Winter?"

"Yes, there's one. The fire watch. Do you know where we can find him?"

Carver's eyebrows raised. "The fire watch? He's not on duty yet, is he? The forestry board said they were deploying him after month-end."

"He's been in the area a week. Greentrees requested that he start earlier because of the fire risk to the wider area. He would have arrived just before the killings started."

Carver looked alarmed. "I've no idea about that. The Forestry Board clearly didn't even think to tell us he was here earlier. I wouldn't know how to find him at all.

Katie swallowed. There was only one possibility. It was dangerous and risky and she didn't know if Carver would agree to it.

"Could we set a fire?" she asked.

His eyes widened in shock. "What? In the forest? No, we can't possibly do that. It's far too risky."

"I wasn't thinking of inside the forest. I was thinking of within the boundaries of the site. You have a whole heap of logs available. And fire extinguishing equipment. What we need to do, is create a trail of smoke that he can see. Because then he will sound the alert. And that will lead us to him."

She waited, holding her breath, to see what Carver would say. Without his agreement, there was no way Katie could go ahead with her plan. And within the next hour, the time they had bought would have gone.

They needed to locate this man, and this was the only way.

CHAPTER THIRTY

Eagle surveyed his territory, his gaze passing over the treetops from his hidden perch. He was alert for any signs of smoke. Always alert.

Years ago, when his mother had passed out drunk, the house had set on fire. Eagle had been trapped on the top floor. Choking, scorched, and with scarring burns on his face and arms, the firemen had eventually rescued him and lifted him out.

He remembered how he'd longed to be able to fly. How flying could have saved him. But nothing had saved him, and after his time in hospital, he had been back home again.

His mother had been in her sixties when she'd died, a ranting, shrunken shell of herself. And yet, Eagle had been her willing servant right until that time. He'd been happy under her rule. Not happy, that was not the right word, but content. He'd served her, obedient and subservient. She had allowed her scarred son to go out and earn. He'd brought home money from the fire watch, to keep them alive.

Then, when she had died, he had finally found the courage to spread his wings. He had discovered who he could really be, and the truth was shocking to him.

He'd never known that this predatory power lay within him, that this ability to kill had been latent, waiting to erupt. A superpower hidden. How amazing that he'd had this all along and had never used it.

Sometimes, he wondered what would have happened if he had plunged his claw-like fingers into his mother's frail body and ended her domineering rule over him earlier. But that was not to wonder, now. All he needed to think about was who else he could kill, in order to ascend to his dream.

The dream of being an airborne predator. Every blood life he took helped him along that road.

Soon, he would reach it.

He began to think about his next victim. Who it would be. The forest was short on pickings now, that he knew. People were scared. But any tall tree would do. He could wait anywhere. The forest was a big place, and people's memories were short.

But for now, his senses were alerted for a different reason. His instincts flared.

His sensitive nose picked it up first. The faint, acrid tang of smoke. Immediately, his head turned.

In all probability it was just a tiny campfire, a camper heating up a pot of stew, warming his hands before wrapping himself in his sleeping bag.

But this was swirling toward him, thicker and darker than the average camping flame.

Eagle felt a strange calmness and power. He raised himself higher in the treetop and looked around. He couldn't see beyond the tallest trees, but undoubtedly, smoke was billowing into the air in an area that he knew was close to the construction site.

Someone's careless cigarette. Some hazard had caused this, and now he was the one who could set it to rights.

It was time to sound the alarm.

Before he did, he felt a sudden, strange moment of hesitation.

Was it right? Was this fire big enough? It seemed strange, for this area. Not like those he'd seen before.

But then, he overcame his doubts. A small fire could grow to a massive conflagration in a moment. He'd seen it many times. Flames could burst and spread. He knew that, from personal experience. He was the one who had watched in horror as his own home erupted into flames, how the coil of smoke had thickened and brightened, consuming the wooden boards greedily.

No, he had to do his job.

Eagle leaped from treetop to treetop, getting close enough to be within earshot.

He took the whistle that hung from a string on his chest and he blew it again and again, as loud as he could.

"Fire!" he screamed. "Fire!" He felt the blood boiling in his veins, the ready beat of his heart.

He reached into his belt pack and took out one of the flares. He lit it, and sent it up. It shot to the sky, letting out a shrill noise and a brightly colored plume of smoke.

His next step was to alert the authorities. Quickly, he sent the messages through with the approximate coordinates of the fire.

Soon, someone would see. Help would arrive. And as soon as that happened, his job was done. He did not have to stick around or get close or do anything further. He could melt away, return to the shadows, to the strange anonymity of his existence, to wait days or weeks or months, for the next fire alarm.

Finally, he saw activity down below in the site and heard the shrill of the alarm. It was very late. They'd taken a while to be alerted. He was surprised by the delay and wondered again if something was amiss.

But that was not his job, to wonder and worry. The fire had been spotted, and he had done what he was paid to do, where his talent lay, or he would never have found himself in this role. He had found his purpose.

He should go now, leave the site. But then another thought struck him.

If he stayed and waited he could find prey, in the chaos. He was sure of it. It would be better to wait, to choose his next victim in the confusion and the smoke.

The fire would mean that people scattered, and when they did, he would be ready to pick the one he wanted.

CHAPTER THIRTY ONE

Katie waited, with her heart in her mouth. Was the fire watch even on site? Would he reveal his whereabouts and was the fire big enough? The small, smoky blaze on the edge of the site was all that Carver had allowed them to build, and it was being strictly monitored by workers with fire extinguishers.

And then she heard the cry, the shrill of the whistle. Then the bright, sudden eruption of a flare.

"He's there?" Carver said in surprise.

There wasn't time to think, no time to do anything but run. Katie had to get to this man.

She had nobody to help her. Carver had insisted that the few people still on site remained behind to control the fire. And in any case, it wasn't right to put civilians in the path of a dangerous criminal. She was in this alone until Leblanc, and police backup, arrived.

Katie wasn't going to be a hero, but she was going to keep track of this man and not allow him to get away.

She raced into the woods, dodging between the trees, following the path that led to the area where he had been watching and waiting. It was impossible to tell which tree he'd been in. On this east-facing slope, it was already almost dark.

She ran through the undergrowth, her breath hissing in and out of her lungs, the branches grabbing at her hair and clothes.

Where was he? Where? He'd been near here. She knew she was close.

Katie paused a moment, and sent Leblanc a pin drop. If she couldn't find the fire watch in these trees, after having seen him actually send up a flare, the chances of him finding her were nonexistent. She hoped he would get here soon, but she couldn't count on him arriving in time. She needed to push forward with this lead, because a man as elusive as this fire watch would find it very easy to disappear if he suspected he was being targeted. Katie couldn't let that happen.

There were so many tall trees here. Which one was it? Where had he sent the flare from? Was it the one ahead, or the next? Now she was wondering if it had been even further away. They all looked the same. In this vast forest, she felt briefly disoriented. At least she had her own pin drop now, to guide her back to her starting point if she did end up moving further through the trees and away from any path.

But she was sure it had been near here. Was that the faintest trace of color in the air, from the flare? With the wind, it was hard to tell.

She put her phone away and moved forward again, aware that the wind was blowing in the wrong direction, and the smoke that was billowing out from the fire was now blocking her view of the treetops and stinging her eyes.

And then, from behind her, she felt the faintest flicker of movement. It was so fast, so sudden, that she had time only to gasp. There was nobody there, and then there was somebody.

Hands, as sharp and rough as claws, grabbed her neck.

Powerfully, inexorably, they wrenched at her throat. The grip was astonishingly strong. In a few moments, Katie knew, her windpipe would be crushed. Already, the air had been choked from her and the blood was pounding in her head.

She could not breathe.

As she struggled to get free, trying to kick and punch the slim figure behind her, she realized that he was like a powerful wild animal. She threw herself backward, desperate to get his hands off her, to dislodge him somehow, but his fingers were like iron bands.

The hands were tightening, crushing the life out of her.

This was like being taken by a predator. That was what it was like, Katie thought. A predator had her. And she couldn't fight him. He was blocking her attempts to reach her gun. One steely arm remained at her throat. The other grabbed her weapon and tossed it away.

Katie's options were narrowing. She didn't want to die here in these woods, to be his last victim. She dreaded the thought of Leblanc finding her in a tree, his trauma, his horror.

But what else could she do?

With all her strength, she threw herself back, but his balance was phenomenal. He didn't so much as stagger, and she was choking now.

What would prey do? The thought crossed her mind. How would a small, harmless mouse manage to survive? How would a helpless victim stay alive?

Play dead, she thought. The trick of every weaker creature everywhere, the last resort, the only solution that was left to her.

Katie allowed a death rattle to escape from her lips and she collapsed in his arms, letting the full weight of her body into his grasp. It felt impossible to force herself to do this, but she had to.

It was her only hope that by doing this, he would let go of her throat before she did, actually, die.

The world went gray. It blanked out. For a while, Katie knew nothing at all.

And then, color and movement returned and she realized, in horror, where she was.

CHAPTER THIRTY TWO

Oxygen trickled into Katie's body, her heart was beating. With a soundless gasp she dragged in air. Her throat was on fire. She was alive, but this fact was of cold comfort as she realized her horrific predicament.

Andrew Hunt, the fire watch man, was dragging her up the tree. She was looking down at the forest, far below, the trees still shrouded in gray smoke. Bark scraped at her hands, which were firmly fastened in one of his.

He was carrying her with ease, but even so, his grasp felt shifting and uncertain and far from secure.

She was slung over his shoulder, face down. With incredible strength and balance, he was heaving himself, and her, from branch to branch. Katie wanted to struggle in terror, but forced herself to stay still.

He was going to dump her. He thought she was dead, and he was going to dump her at the top of this tree. A sick fear surged in her as she imagined what it would take to do that. What if she fell? If she didn't fall, how could she escape him?

She wasn't tied, that was the only advantage. But she was at his mercy, because if she began to struggle, all he would have to do was to drop her.

She'd fall sixty, seventy feet, head first. It would be lethal. Her stomach twisted at the thought. The forest looked tiny below her. They were impossibly high in the air. She was his prisoner, his prey. Any struggle could see them both toppling out of this tree and on a terrifying journey to annihilation below.

How could she save herself? Perhaps she should just wait until he arranged her at the top. If her nerve held enough for her to do that. She didn't even want to think what that would take. What would it take, to keep limp, while a madman tried to shove her into the fork of a tree, more than seventy feet high?

It was her only option, Katie decided. It would be more than a test of her courage. She didn't know if she'd manage, but she had to try. If he could get her there, he would then leave her be.

But then, he spoke, a breathy whisper, words that were clearly meant for him, and him alone.

"This time, I will release my prey, she will fall. She will fall and I will fly."

Katie gasped in shock. She'd been right in that this damaged man was on a mission, and he was taking things a step further. Now, instead of creating a nest, he was going to launch her from the top of the tree, believing – somehow – that her fall would give him the power he needed.

She would plummet to her death. So would he, but it would be too late for her.

What could she do? She had only a minute to save herself.

The only answer that Katie could think of was that she'd have to wait until she saw the right branch. When she did, she'd have to hook her foot under it, and try to jerk herself out of his grasp.

It was going to be intensely risky, but she didn't see another way. And they were nearly at the top of the tree. The branches were thinner. There was not much time left before it was too late.

She'd have to take a chance. That branch, there.

Katie lashed out her leg, curling it over the branch, trying to wrench herself away from him.

The element of surprise was on her side. He gasped, and his grasp on her loosened.

Yelling in horror, her voice hoarse, Katie wrenched a hand free, and made a desperate grab for the branch, jackknifing her body away from him.

"No!" he yelled, his voice furious. He made a grab for her, his hands as strong and sharp as claws. He had her. He was going to capture her again.

Desperately, tugging at the branch with all her might, she jerked away from him, knowing this was her only chance, feeling a flare of fear that the action might loosen her own handhold and send her falling to the ground far below.

But she managed. She tore free of him, even though the action almost caused her to fall, her hands slipping on the bark.

Sobbing with the effort, Katie grasped the branch with both hands and writhed away from him, desperately lowering herself, knowing speed would be her only salvation. But the smoke was stinging her eyes and blocking her view. This was so dangerous. They were so high. The branches were flimsy and this was his hunting ground, not hers.

And he was coming after her.

With a shout of anger, he swung down. He was so fast, so powerful. He was going to catch up with her in a moment.

She reached out, grabbing hold of another, lower branch. But the branch was too thin. It broke under her. And then he was there, roaring in rage, pushing her off the tree. Her grasp was dislodged, her footing was gone.

Katie screamed in horror as she began to fall.

It was over. She had lost the battle, there was no more purchase for her to hold onto. The spindly branch burned her palm as it slipped through. Now, there would be nothing. Only a rush of empty air, the stomach-twisting fall, the wind rushing past her. Nothing more, until the agonizing impact with the ground.

And then, from below, a hand grabbed her and clung on hard.

"I've got you! I've got you!"

Fingers closed tightly, holding her firm. It was Leblanc. She clung to him, gasping for breath, wrapping her other arm around a branch, feeling her entire body shaking.

At the last minute, he'd saved her. He'd gotten the message, and the coordinates. He must have heard her screams and the sound of the struggle. He'd climbed up the tree in time to save her.

"I've got you," he said, his voice sounding as shaky as she felt. "The police are below. They're here. He won't get away."

"He's still fighting," Katie said, her voice wobbly. She was sure that her captor was now going to try and send them both to the forest floor.

"Come down from here," she appealed to him. It was weird to be talking to him, with his face just a yard away from hers, staring into the eyes of a man who had tried to murder her just a few minutes ago.

"You need to climb down the tree and give yourself up to the police," Leblanc said harshly. He was still holding tightly to Katie, as she adjusted her grip on the branch, feeling another wave of dizziness which she guessed was as much from the lack of oxygen she'd experienced, as from the height they were at.

"I'm not coming down. You'll never have me." Hunt laughed, a tight, brittle sound.

"This tree is surrounded by police. You're not getting away," Leblanc said firmly.

Katie felt a momentary fear in her stomach because what if he still could? He was as agile as an acrobat up there in the branches. He could leap to another tree and be lost in the coiling smoke. Or he could try something else, a different, deadlier tactic.

She heard a tearing noise and the next moment, Katie ducked as a branch swished past her head.

Fear flamed inside her as she realized he'd broken it off and thrown it down. He wasn't giving up. He wanted to send them both plummeting to their death.

Leblanc cried out and she twisted around, staring down, worry filling her. Had he been hurt? This was way too high for any good outcome if either of them lost their grip.

The fear of falling clenched at her again. An instinctive fear. She grasped her support branch tighter. It felt reassuringly rough and solid – if she didn't think of the endless drop to the ground below. Leblanc couldn't dare to get his gun out now, not when he needed to hold on with both hands to ensure his stability.

Another branch crashed past them. A twig from it scratched Katie's face and she twisted away.

She felt below her with her foot.

Fighting was not the answer here. The only solution was to run, and the only way was down. The further they climbed away from him, the closer they got to the police, the harder it would be for him to follow. But there were no branches within easy reach. They needed time to feel their way further down, time they didn't have.

"I've got a sight on him!"

The words came from below and they filled Katie with relief. One of the men on the ground must have gotten a clear view for a moment, in the blowing smoke.

"Don't move!" he shouted. "I can get him without danger to you. I'll take him down!"

"Copy that!" Katie yelled back, keeping as still as possible, bracing herself for the whiplash sound of the shot.

But then, the man above them turned to stare at her and she saw a strange expression in his empty, pale eyes. It wasn't the expression she'd expected to see. Rather than defiance, she saw a moment of pure, mad joy in his eyes.

"It's time," he cried out.

To her astonishment, he launched himself out of the tree, for a moment, as graceful and elegant as a bird taking flight.

A moment later, gravity took hold. With a cry, he plummeted to the ground, limbs flailing.

He landed with a crash and a crackle of branches. She heard him groaning.

"He's alive. Injured, but alive. We have him," she heard the police shout.

Katie stared at Leblanc. He was still gripping her hand tightly. Never had she felt more terrified, or more alive.

They had done it. They had caught one of the most evil and elusive killers she'd ever pursued. And it meant that they had saved themselves. They'd met the governor's impossible conditions. He could not go back on his promise. Their unit would live on, with full autonomy.

Katie began the difficult, dangerous climb back to the ground.

As she lowered herself carefully down the branches, she thought of what it had taken to get this man.

A shift in her thinking. A revisiting of the facts. And a determination not to give up.

If she did the same with her sister's whereabouts, Katie wondered if she could find her this time.

EPILOGUE

Katie strode across the broken, rocky trail. There was a chill in the air, despite the weak sun glimmering through the clouds.

The world around her looked stark and empty. She was trying again. Trying to find Gabriel Rath, but this time, reinterpreting what she'd been told. There was a town in New York called Clare. That was what she had thought he meant.

But on the Canadian side, not too far away, there was a town called Clarins.

And it was all too possible that Gabriel Rath had taken her here, and that Mrs. Ingham had misheard the name of the town, or else Rath had deliberately changed it.

Katie had looked on the map. Looked carefully. And she had seen the small knot of woods that she'd noticed in the photo. The difference was that this time, it looked identical.

She was trying again. On her own. She had nothing to lose now, nothing at all.

Whatever it took, she had to try. If he was not here, she would give up, because it would mean her last lead had fizzled out and she should accept her father's words, and try to make peace with her parents again, knowing that she, too, must give up any hope of ever seeing Josie again.

She would accept the search was over and that Gabriel had managed to outwit her, to move, to escape anyone who might try to follow.

But she had to try this first, because she could have gotten it wrong. And if she'd gotten it wrong and didn't try to get it right, she'd never forgive herself.

If she hadn't tried that same strategy in the recent case, the case that had saved the task force, they would never have found the fire watch.

Katie clung to that belief as she headed toward the area where the forested hide was, where Gabriel's cabin might be. In her mind, she was trying to accept the fact it would probably not be there, that this was a last-ditch attempt, that he would be long gone, or else that she was looking in the wrong place.

If this was a mistake, she would be able to walk away, she said to herself. But if he was here, she would find him. Failing would be too terrifying a price to pay.

As she got closer to the woods, her heart was thumping and her chest was tight with the need to achieve her goal.

She turned off the trail and into the dense, dark growth. It took her a few moments to make out the path she was on. She was trying not to think of the potential for failure. She could not allow herself that.

And then, she saw it. Buried in the gloomy woods. Its boards were darker than she'd expected, oiled or painted so that they were barely discernible against the darkness of the pines.

His cabin. She rushed toward it, her heart in her throat. It was here! The map had been correct. The town name had been wrong, but otherwise, it had led her accurately to its very doorstep.

But at the door, she stopped. She felt paralyzed by indecision. She realized she had not thought that far ahead. What would she do if she found him?

Was he inside?

She knocked, but there was no response.

"Can I come in?" she called.

She took hold of the door handle, wondering if she had the courage to turn it, and push it open.

Of course she did. She'd come this far and there was no turning back. Now, she had to see what was inside, if anything was. And as she turned it, it opened. Hinges shrilled. The door, swollen from rain, ground against the boards below as she pushed it back.

She stepped into the interior. It smelled of smoke and sweat and old food. It was rustic, with a rough floor and raw, basic wooden furniture.

And there was a shape at the far end, looming in the darkness, turning to her with triumph and rage in his eyes.

Katie cried out as she saw him. He was there! Gabriel Rath. He'd been waiting for her inside, silent, aggressive. She couldn't believe it. Adrenaline flooded her, making it seem for a moment as if time slowed down and it was just the two of them, standing there, staring at each other, as if the meeting had been preordained for years and was finally playing out.

His eyes were wide in his weathered face. His hair and beard were longer and wilder than she remembered, now heavily streaked with gray.

147

"I've been looking for you. For a long time," she stammered out. "I hope you don't mind me coming in here. May I speak to you?"

All she could hear in response was the harsh rasp of his breathing.

"I've come here to ask you some questions. You remember me? Where's my sister? Where's Josie?" Her voice shook with tension. It didn't sound like her own voice at all.

But as shocked as she was, Katie realized he wasn't going to give any answers. That was not why he'd allowed her to enter his dark domain. Instead, his face contorted. With a roar of fury, he picked something up from the sideboard. In the dark, Katie only caught a glimpse of it. It was a long, steel knife, sharp and lethal.

He raised it high, and he launched himself at her.

"I've been waiting for you," he roared. "I knew you'd get here one day! And now, I'm going to kill you!"

Katie jumped back, her reactions saving her from the flashing blade as it came down toward her. She grabbed his arm, but he was thrusting it up and forward, trying to drive it into her, fighting to stab her to death.

He was a huge man. Muscled. With a strength that was terrifying. And Katie realized that he was fully intending to kill her.

She had to stop him at once. She was aware she was no match for him. He lashed her hand away as if it was nothing more than a stick. She managed to dive out of the path of the blade, but she tumbled backward over the low bench, her feet flying up in the air as she landed heavily on her back.

She cried out at the pain. Adrenaline coursed through her and she struggled to get up, but he was on top of her, the knife flashing near her face.

She tried to grab his hand, but he was too strong.

"No! Please, don't do this! There's no need!" she begged him, but he was intent on his mission.

"I'm going to kill you, Katie Winter. I've been waiting for years," he threatened in a low, rough, breathless voice.

If she didn't act, if she didn't surprise him and throw him off course, there would be no time, and he'd be able to do what he'd been planning to do for longer than she'd realized.

Next to the bench was a rustic stool. Katie grabbed hold of its wooden base and flung it at Gabriel. It flew into him, knocking him off balance, and as he flailed, she twisted backward, trying to get away from him.

She needed to get to her gun. It was all that could save her now, and she had only a moment before he attacked again.

Katie grabbed it out of the holster and aimed, taking care to wing him, to hit him in the arm. She wanted to disable his lethal force but could not afford to take a killing shot.

She squeezed the trigger.

But as she did, with a cry, he leaped straight into the path of the gun.

The bullet took him square in the chest, and Katie gasped as he fell, crashing to the ground. Blood pumped onto the boards. He groaned in pain and astonishment, but the sound was soft and fractured.

She dove forward, desperately trying to stem the flow, but it was too late, he was dying. His hand scrabbled vainly at the bench, the fingers weak.

"Where is she? Where?" Katie screamed at him. "Where is she?"

For a moment, it seemed Gabriel would answer her. His eyes met hers. His lips moved, breathing words she could not hear.

She leaned closer, grabbing him hard, feeling her hands wet with blood.

And then, his eyes rolled back in his head.

He was gone. Gone.

Katie howled in despair. He had died, despite all she'd done, her best efforts. She'd never wanted to kill him, never intended to do so. Guilt flared inside her at the defensive actions he'd forced her to take, and the loss this represented. He'd died, and with him went his secrets. Now, she would never know where Josie was, or what he had done with her. Never!

Katie scrambled up, sobbing, stamping her foot on the floor in a frenzy of grief. She would never know now. All she could do was to shout and stamp out her sadness, here in this isolated place, where nobody could see or hear.

But the floor felt hollow. Her stamp seemed to echo around the cabin. It was as if the board flexed slightly under her tread.

Could it be? Could it?

She didn't even allow herself to hope as she grabbed the discarded knife and forced its blade between a crack in the planks. She didn't know what she was wishing for. She was too terrified, too traumatized even to wish as she pried up this plank, next to the dead body of the man who had tried to kill her.

And a space appeared before her eyes. A massive, dark, stinking space, hollowed deep into the cold earth.

Katie's eyes narrowed at the fetid smell that rushed out. Quickly, she got the flashlight off her belt, and with shaking hands, turned it on.

Coldness filled her as the beam illuminated a pair of eyes in the darkness far below.

Terrified eyes.

Wide, green eyes that she recognized.

Impossibly, unbelievably, what she had been seeking was here.

"Josie?" she whispered. "Is that you?"

NOW AVAILABLE!

REMEMBER ME
(A Katie Winter FBI Suspense Thriller—Book 9)

When a body is found gruesomely impaled on a tree in a frozen landscape, FBI Special Agent Katie Winter must team up with her partner to enter this killer's mind. But the case leads her down a rabbit hole deeper—and more dangerous—than she ever could have expected.

"Molly Black has written a taut thriller that will keep you on the edge of your seat... I absolutely loved this book and can't wait to read the next book in the series!"
—Reader review for Girl One: Murder

REMEMBER ME is book #9 in a new series by #1 bestselling mystery and suspense author Molly Black.

FBI Special Agent Katie Winter is no stranger to frigid winters, isolation, and dangerous cases. With her sterling record of hunting down serial killers, she is a fast-rising star in the BAU, and Katie is the natural choice to partner with Canadian law enforcement to track killers across brutal and unforgiving landscapes.

A page-turning and harrowing crime thriller featuring a brilliant and tortured FBI agent, the KATIE WINTER series is a riveting mystery, packed with non-stop action, suspense, twists and turns, revelations, and driven by a breakneck pace that will keep you flipping pages late into the night. Fans of Rachel Caine, Teresa Driscoll and Robert Dugoni are sure to fall in love.

Future books in the series will be available soon!

"I binge read this book. It hooked me in and didn't stop till the last few pages... I look forward to reading more!"

—Reader review for Found You

"I loved this book! Fast-paced plot, great characters and interesting insights into investigating cold cases. I can't wait to read the next book!"
—Reader review for Girl One: Murder

"Very good book… You will feel like you are right there looking for the kidnapper! I know I will be reading more in this series!"
—Reader review for Girl One: Murder

"This is a very well written book and holds your interest from page 1… Definitely looking forward to reading the next one in the series, and hopefully others as well!"
—Reader review for Girl One: Murder

"Wow, I cannot wait for the next in this series. Starts with a bang and just keeps going."
—Reader review for Girl One: Murder

"Well written book with a great plot, one that will keep you up at night. A page turner!"
—Reader review for Girl One: Murder

"A great suspense that keeps you reading… can't wait for the next in this series!"
—Reader review for Found You

"Sooo soo good! There are a few unforeseen twists… I binge read this like I binge watch Netflix. It just sucks you in."
—Reader review for Found You

Molly Black

Bestselling author Molly Black is author of the MAYA GRAY FBI suspense thriller series, comprising nine books (and counting); of the RYLIE WOLF FBI suspense thriller series, comprising six books (and counting); of the TAYLOR SAGE FBI suspense thriller series, comprising six books (and counting); and of the KATIE WINTER FBI suspense thriller series, comprising nine books (and counting).

An avid reader and lifelong fan of the mystery and thriller genres, Molly loves to hear from you, so please feel free to visit www.mollyblackauthor.com to learn more and stay in touch.

BOOKS BY MOLLY BLACK

MAYA GRAY MYSTERY SERIES
GIRL ONE: MURDER (Book #1)
GIRL TWO: TAKEN (Book #2)
GIRL THREE: TRAPPED (Book #3)
GIRL FOUR: LURED (Book #4)
GIRL FIVE: BOUND (Book #5)
GIRL SIX: FORSAKEN (Book #6)
GIRL SEVEN: CRAVED (Book #7)
GIRL EIGHT: HUNTED (Book #8)
GIRL NINE: GONE (Book #9)

RYLIE WOLF FBI SUSPENSE THRILLER
FOUND YOU (Book #1)
CAUGHT YOU (Book #2)
SEE YOU (Book #3)
WANT YOU (Book #4)
TAKE YOU (Book #5)
DARE YOU (Book #6)

TAYLOR SAGE FBI SUSPENSE THRILLER
DON'T LOOK (Book #1)
DON'T BREATHE (Book #2)
DON'T RUN (Book #3)
DON'T FLINCH (Book #4)
DON'T REMEMBER (Book #5)
DON'T TELL (Book #6)

KATIE WINTER FBI SUSPENSE THRILLER
SAVE ME (Book #1)
REACH ME (Book #2)
HIDE ME (Book #3)
BELIEVE ME (Book #4)
HELP ME (Book #5)
FORGET ME (Book #6)
HOLD ME (Book #7)
PROTECT ME (Book #8)

REMEMBER ME (Book #9)